For Teacher Nancy, Mrs. Meadows, and Mrs. Saunders.

Acknowledgments

FIRST OF ALL, I WOULD like to thank the Lord Almighty for giving me the creative ability to write this book and the many more to come.

I also want to thank my parents, who pushed me to write in the third grade and encouraged me in the seventh and every grade in between. Thank you, Mrs. Tredick, for recommending me to be in the GATE program. Thanks be to my fifth-grade teacher Mrs. Pithey, for listening to the story I had written during recess, lunch, and after school. I thank Mrs. Hubbard, my sixth-grade teacher, for encouraging me to write and telling the class how to write an "About the Author" page. Thank you, Mrs. Meadows and Mrs. Saunders of Sierra Vista Jr. High, for encouraging me about the bookmark contest. I want to thank Teacher Nancy and the rest of the TCOTWSC teachers and pastors I know for teaching me about the Lord Almighty. Thank you, Mrs. Fulleman, for letting me work on my story in the school library. And thank you, Iulie, for being my friend. Also, I want to thank Bryan Davis for writing the books that helped inspire me to begin writing.

Pronunciation Guide

Alseka: al-SAKE-a
Alexion: al-X-ee-on
Alexiov: al-X-ee-OV
Bengial: ben-GE-all
Barnillon: bar-NILL-on
Barshal: BAR-shawl
Caredest: CARE-a-DES-t
Ceriphina: Sara-FEEN-a
Emayne: e-MAINE
Enstar: ON-star
Exposial: ex-POSE-ee-all
Ilde: ILL-d
Lindsair: lind-SAYER
Marsara: MAR-sar-a
Masseran: MASS-er-ANN
Milikitea: mil-ick-a-TAE-a
Moraiha: more-AYE-a
Norheil: nor-HEEL
Oeilla: OY-ella
Ruofen: ROOF-en
Ralloy: RALL-oy
Rythan: RYE-than
Thias: THEE-as
Setlia: set-LEE-a

Zaphn: ZAPH-n
Zerhal: zer-HAL
Zinnune: ZINN-une
Zynkosiac: ZIN-coze-i-ack

Chapter 1

Anger

I TIPTOED, FOLLOWING MY OLDER brother into my friend Ralloy's living room. Someone had shouted in the early morning, and I wanted to know who he was. Neither Ralloy or his dad yelled at three in the morning. So something must be wrong.

My brother stopped. "Oiella isn't here," he whispered. I peeked around him, noticing for the first time that the little Zyncosiac, with her white fur and silver bands around her arms, legs, and tail and delicate wings, wasn't at her usual sleeping spot on the couch. Strange. Oiella always slept soundly there.

"Sane? Ceriphina? What are you doing here this early?" I heard behind us. I turned and saw Ralloy's mom, Emayne, in her pajamas. Her eyes were red from shedding tears, and her face was flushed.

"We heard someone shout over here, so we thought we would come and see what was wrong," Sane explained. "Where's Oiella?"

Emayne sniffled. "She was gone when Ruofen woke up. As well as the EIC Ralloy was keeping, and…" she trailed

9

off. "Come upstairs and I'll show you." Emayne then walked to the stairs and climbed up. My brother looked at me, and we followed her, wondering what could be missing on the second floor of Ralloy's home.

We reached the top as seven-year-old Ralloy burst from his sister Marsara's room, tears streaming down his face. He rushed into his room and slammed the door. I could hear him yelling, shouting at the top of his lungs. I stepped towards Ralloy's room, confused at why he was crying. Ralloy didn't cry much.

A strong hand settled on my shoulder, bigger than Sane's. "Ceriph ... please, don't go in Ralloy's room right now." Ruofen, Ralloy's dad said gently.

I turned around and looked at his sad face. Suddenly, I was afraid. Ruofen cried less than Ralloy. The last time he had shed a tear was over a year ago. What could have happened to make the whole family sorrowful? And why wasn't Marsara awake yet?

"Ceriph? You ... you need to see this." Sane's voice trembled. I walked hesitantly over to the door of my friend's room and looked inside.

Marsara's bed was messy, but she wasn't there. She wasn't in her room. A capital letter B was carved into the wall above her nightstand.

"Wh ... where's Marsara?" I asked Ruofen quietly.

"We don't know, Ceriph." Ralloy's dad said. "She was taken."

Later that day, I was walking to school with my brother Sane. Ralloy had been avoiding us ever since the early morning. Everyone in our mountain city of Varnillon now knew what had happened, and Ruofen had gotten a little more information about who had taken her. I looked up as we passed a sign that asked if anyone had seen Marsara. There was a name written on it, *Barnillon*, the group that Ruofen suspected had kidnapped his daughter. He also thought that they might be a special division of the neighboring nation Alseka's Oppressionist armies. I caught a glance at another poster of an unfamiliar person, but paid no attention to it.

Ralloy wasn't just sad. He was *angry* at this Barnillon, at the enemy Alseka. They never said sorry, and Marsara wasn't home yet. Maybe he had a right to be mad, but maybe Ralloy was taking it a little far? Perhaps he didn't mean it, but it hurt, how he wasn't with us.

Today was my birthday. Today, Ralloy passed me by without a glance. As I blew out the six candles on my small cake made by my brother, I wished that Ralloy would soon stop being angry and be friends with us again.

A couple of years passed. It was Friday, but there wasn't any school because someone thought the Oppression was coming. Probably a false alarm, as it had happened before over the years, and there had been no attacks. Just that Terrible Raid, as people called it.

Sane walked into my room, his four-year-old scabbard with a gleaming sword inside thwapping against his leg. "Hey, Ceriph," he greeted me.

"Hey," I said back. I looked out the window, wistfully, at Ralloy's house.

"Ralloy got accepted into soldier training today. Early. Maybe his dad helped." he walked over and put a hand on my hair the color of golden flax. "As soon as he's ready, he will wage war against the Barnillion and get Marsara back," he said, laughing nervously at his joke. It wasn't a joke, though. Ralloy still was angry at the loss of his sister. Sane was telling the truth.

Four years and eleven months later, I sat on a chair, on a warning day, waiting for Sane to return from training. He always had a break at lunch, and he usually left before I woke up to get a chance to talk to Ralloy. However, eleven o'clock came and went with no sign of Sane. I waited a little more, hoping that my brother was just late or in the middle of a sudden mock battle. But the minutes piled up, and I knew that it was taking too long for either of those options.

There was a knock at the door. I jumped up, hoping it might be Sane. I disarmed the alarm, then removed the deadbolt, then deactivated the triple-encrypted lock. Finally, the door opened, revealing Ruofen's concerned face. My shoulders sagged a little, but it wasn't often that Ruofen visited.

"Is Sane sick today? He didn't come to training." he told me.

"He didn't? I thought he was there," I responded. Suddenly, I felt the blood drain from my face. If Sane wasn't at training, then did he ever get out of bed? Had something happened during the night?

I turned around and ran up the stairs to Sane's room, terrified to think of what happened, but afraid to not know the truth. I made the right turn and stopped.

The door was ajar, one of the hinges broken. I peeked around it and gasped.

Sane's room was messy, as if there had been a battle there. His sword was stuck in the wall. His scabbard and belt were on his messed-up bed. There was a human-sized dent in the wall near the embedded blade. Shirts were strewn around the room. His soldier's uniform was hanging from the ceiling fan.

Sane wasn't there. Like Marsara, my seventeen-year-old brother had been taken.

Exactly seven years after the Terrible Raid, I silenced my bedside alarm. Another attack alert, so no school today. "Happy birthday to me," I muttered, but it wasn't happy at all. November first, seven years ago, had been the saddest day of my life. And now, I was alone.

I got out of bed and dressed. Every day, I had hoped that Ralloy would be calm. Every day, my hope was shattered. Yet I still would not give up on Ralloy. He was my friend. So every day, I hoped that his raging bonfire had been diminished by even a little bit. I kept that in mind as I had breakfast, brushed my teeth, and crossed the street to Ralloy's house.

Perhaps Ralloy would talk today. Perhaps my hope would today be fulfilled.

Chapter 2

Then I Got Lost

"Oh, Ruofen brought Ralloy on an assignment to investigate a tunnel in the mountain in the Razorwood grove. They left fifteen minutes ago." Emayne stood at the door and told me.

I sighed. "It figures. He's been doing assignments like this for five weeks."

"Yes, yes, he has. However, I'm a little worried, Ceriphina, about why. I know Ralloy said that he would let go of his anger, but … everyone knows that it's no easy task to line up actions with words …" she trailed off.

"But shouldn't we at least be seeing *improvement*?" I finished for her. "What I mean is, he changed his behavior. But he just … doesn't seem *better*. I don't even see him anymore, not even in the *window!*" I crossed my arms and sighed in frustration. Ralloy avoiding me was one thing that I did not like very much. The past seven years were bad enough, talking to him once every three months or so, up until five weeks ago. It really made no sense. Ralloy kept his promises … usually. At least, seven years ago, as far as I remember.

It really doesn't feel like he's keeping this promise, except that Ralloy really didn't promise anything. Which isn't very promising.

"Okay, I'll let it go, Sane! I'll forget the Terrible Raid even happened!"

After Ralloy, my adopted older brother Sane, and I had finally been able to talk, Sane wanted to know if Ralloy would stop being angry, because he was injuring himself and others around him. When he asked, though, Ralloy practically exploded. Sane tried to calm him down, but the situation escalated quickly, ending with Ralloy storming out of the room. I haven't seen him since.

Ralloy really *didn't* promise anything.

"Go ahead and follow them," Emayne said.

"Sure, I'll follow them," I agreed. I jumped of the porch and began jogging down the street.

"Uh, Ceriphina? Ralloy and Ruofen went the *other* way," Emayne corrected me. I stopped and turned around.

"Oops. Thanks for telling me," I said and walked in the other direction.

"Just helping," Ralloy's mother replied. "Stay safe, Ceriphina."

"I will." I answered as I turned the corner.

Fifteen minutes later, I was tiptoeing in the Razorwood grove, the small brush forest that hugged the mountain's peak. I hadn't seen either Ruofen or Ralloy yet.

Hopefully, Ralloy and Ruofen aren't following me *now. Because that would be ironic.*

I stood still and cautiously looked around. The Razorwood trees were holding up some of the snow from the storm last night, but most of it got through and blanketed the grove. As I looked around, I didn't recognize anything. The fact that I wasn't here much—not at all—really didn't help.

Panicky glances told of trees, trees, and more Razorwood trees on every side. Until I spotted a dome-shaped tree several trees away. An acacia tree.

But the last time I checked, acacia trees didn't grow on snowy mountains. They grew on *savannas*, which this clearly is not. So this should be interesting.

I carefully jogged quickly over to the acacia tree. But as I examined it, I got the feeling that something was wrong about it. And not just the geographic location.

"It's not real," I heard from behind me. I turned around and stared.

There was a man there. He had an African build, which characterized the people of Zerhal in the Far North. The man was looking at me. His blue long-sleeved shirt assured his Zerhali origin. A thin yellow lightning bolt dominating over a winding subtle purple streak was emblazoned on it. A small lightning bolt sat in the upper left corner. That was the symbol of Zerhali royalty, but soldiers could also wear it in the Zerhali military. The man held a wooden sword even though he had a suitable scabbard for it. But why was his sword made of wood?

"Who are you?" I asked. "And how can you tell?"

The man walked over to the acacia tree. "I don't think that this type of tree can grow in this climate," he answered.

I knew that.

"Then what's it made of?" I asked.

The man tapped his wooden sword against the acacia tree. Instead of what I would assume to be was the sound of wood on wood, the sword hit metal. "Some type of metal.

To produce something this realistic, it's probably cybersteel," he replied.

"Okay ..." I reached and touched the acacia tree. It felt like a tree, but it was cold and hard, like metal. The man was right.

"What are you doing here? This is not a comfortable place, especially when it's cold," the Zerhali man asked.

"I ... uh, well ... I was looking for my ... neighbor ... and his dad. But I got lost," I told him. Funny, though. I always thought of Ralloy as my friend, or half like it, but that wasn't reality. A friend wouldn't avoid me. But still, in my head, he was my friend. Like he was seven years ago.

"Oh. Why do you have to look for him?" he asked me. It seemed like a silly question, as it was obvious to me. Apparently, my situation is *not* obvious.

"Because he's *avoiding* me," I answered. That really felt like a teenager line.

"Hmm," the man said. "Why would you want to be with someone who is avoiding you?" the man asked.

Hmm. Good question.

"It's complicated ..." I answered simply.

"I have time," he replied. Then he sat on a rock that was partially covered in snow. I squatted.

I only got to Ralloy's name when the man stiffened and looked at the sky. I turned and peered too.

It was still cloudy, but now I could hear faintly the sound of a downbeat. The fact that the Zerhali man could hear that while I was speaking proved that he was definitely an experienced warrior. Not exactly comforting when I saw what he was seeing.

The clouds obscured most of it, but I was certain of what they hid.

An Exposial dragon. A well-known species on Setlia, but one I would have never expected to see. Despite the ever-growing chances of a war between Caredest and Alseka, the mega-nation—no, *world dominator*—that literally *bordered* Caredest to the southwest. Even though I lived on the mountain that was smack on top of that border. I just never thought about it. I was more concerned about Ralloy than the impending war.

Suddenly, the fifteen-foot-tall white bulk of Exposial dragon pointed its head to the ground only several feet away from the man and me. As it began descending, I wondered if the Exposial had spotted me or the lone Zerhali warrior. The presence of one was suspicious by itself since there was no war at the current moment—not only suspicion, but it was a threat. Exposial dragons were strong and powerful. It was a thing no one wanted to get cornered by one.

Because they were Oppressionists.

The Exposial dragon landed on his hind feet. He looked around, but he didn't see us. I slowly retreated behind the fake acacia tree to make sure it stayed that way.

As the dragon turned his head and long five-foot neck again, I caught sight of a black "smudge" on his left cheek. The cold fear I already felt multiplied by a thousand because that "smudge" wasn't a smudge.

It was a burn scar.

Only *one* Exposial dragon had that *specific* burn scar. And he was not only their leader, he was perhaps the most dangerous of them all.

For this Exposial dragon was well-known. The news never really biased on this, but he was definitely *infamous*. This dragon was named Zaphn.

The man, now joining me behind the tree, take deep breaths. I was hyperventilating in contrast. It was relieving, as deep breathes meant that he was not going to attack Zaphn. That would end terribly.

But Zaphn did not turn to us or even acknowledged we were there. As if we didn't even *exist*.

I didn't drop my guard, however. It was something Ralloy told me before the Terrible Raid commenced. Back when we were real friends, before he was avoiding me.

"Don't ever drop your guard when someone or something you don't trust is nearby, Ceriph. Promise?"

I had promised him that, over seven years ago. So I kept my guard up.

Zaphn looked around some more in complete silence. Then he gave a powerful downbeat and took to the air.

And then Zaphn surprised me.

He looked straight at me through the fake tree branches. His look shocked me. His look said he knew we were there the whole time … but he didn't attack. Why? Because imminent war was too premature to begin now?

The Exposial dragon swiftly flew out of sight as my mind tried processing what just happened.

A full minute passed before the Zerhali warrior spoke.

"That … was a first," he said.

"Seeing an Exposial outside of battle or him knowing we were there and sparing us?" I asked. The man shrugged as a response. We stood there for another minute, then the Zerhali man walked around the tree and stopped at Zaphn's imprints on the snow. I walked over to him.

"Is now the best time for an introduction?" the man asked politely.

"I'm sure that there have been better times," I replied. Then I told him my name.

"A nice name, Ceriphina. It fits such a fair maiden as you," the man stated gently and thoughtfully.

My face felt hot. "I really don't know if I've done anything to prove that," I said. I knew he wasn't talking about looks.

The man turned to face me, a little awkwardly. "And … let me tell you my name. I am Augustine."

Chapter 3

Augustine

WAIT. *AUGUSTINE?*

Augustine was the elder son of the king of Zerhal. Augustine was the expected heir to the throne of the Arctic nation. But he wasn't. His father declared his younger brother Zinnune the heir, and Augustine was the heir-not-to-be. Nobody knew why the Zerhali king chose Zinnune over Augustine except the king himself and the Lord Almighty. Not even Augustine himself, because he had almost caused a Zerhali civil war because he had wanted the throne.

And then both brothers went incognito after that ... at least until now. To say that I was surprised was an understatement.

I stared at a man who had torn his family to shreds. Augustine wanted to be the king of Zerhal, and the already fragile nation had almost collapsed as a result. He had done so much.

But was that the same man who stood before me now?

The Augustine in front of me held a wooden sword, not the sword of the Zerhali heir. This Augustine seemed ... well, softer from what I knew him to be. From what I had heard.

Augustine looked at me gently. He gazed at me as if he were pleading for a pardon. He knew I knew what he had done to Zerhal, but he had acted as if it hadn't happened. At least before he told me his name. I was looking into the eyes of a man who felt the heavy load of guilt. Augustine's eyes told me that he was sorry. And then we were interrupted suddenly by a yell. The sound surprised me. I looked to the right and began running toward it. I recognized the voice as Ralloy's.

My feet stumbled on tree roots as I heard Ruofen shouting for Ralloy to stop. I pressed on, step after step after step, until my legs felt like fire. Finally, I collapsed on the bare edge of a large clearing and caught my breath.

When I looked up, I saw Ruofen stepping back. A guy dressed as a guard held a sword to Augustine's chest. The guard looked shocked as if the heir-not-to-be came out of nowhere and prevented him from wounding Ruofen.

Then again, that probably *was* what happened.

But Augustine was not unprotected. He held his wooden sword with both hands and was lifting his opponent's blade up to his neck.

Wait, but that was *more* dangerous. If the guard pushed his blade any further, Augustine would be severely wounded.

The guard apparently realized that, because he braced himself and began applying more pressure on his sword.

But in a split second, Augustine moved his sword in a way that he disarmed the guard and held his wooden sword point in the same position as his opponent had done on him.

A silence followed. The guard looked shaken, then yelled in panic and ran to a tunnel in the mountainside that edged the clearing.

When I looked back at Augustine, I noticed, even from five feet away, that his sword was trembling. Then he dropped it in the snow.

Ruofen appeared to be speechless. It wasn't every day that he gets his life saved by a stranger. No one present in Varnillon currently had seen Augustine before. That was why I needed his name to recognize him.

Then I heard the ring of metal against metal inside the tunnel. Ruofen immediately turned and ran toward the sound. I stayed put and continued to watch Augustine. Saving a stranger and purposely putting himself at risk were not the marks of an insensitive person.

Something had happened. Something had changed since Augustine disappeared. But I didn't know *what.*

Augustine stood still. Then he slowly knelt and grasped the hilt of his wooden sword. Then he fingered the hilt of the other sword, the one he had forced out of the guard's hand. He stared at it for a while.

Another yell snapped him out of it, and he got up and ran to the tunnel. He left the sword behind.

I stood up and walked over to the sword. As I examined it, wondering why Augustine turned down the better sword, I noticed a crude engraving on the base of the blade. When I looked even closer, the engraving proved to form a *B.*

It didn't take very long for me to piece things together regarding the guard. He was from the Barnillon.

And there was no telling what he would do when he got there.

I picked up the sword. It was heavier than I had expected. It was all I could do with it, dragging it on the snow to the tunnel. When I got to the tunnel, I dropped it. As it clanged on the stone floor, I looked at the tunnel's descent into the depths of Mount Thias. It extended past the light, down, down, down ... I couldn't begin to guess what lay before me.

The echo of swords clanging against each other made me jittery. Should I go and figure out what was happening? Or should I go back to Varnillon and tell Emayne what I knew?

A look behind me told me that the second option was impossible, as I was most certainly lost. That left me to either stay put and panic and whatever or go on into the tunnel.

Panicking is not a favorite pastime of mine, so I marched into the tunnel and began down the stairs with no real purpose at this point aside from finding Ralloy, Ruofen, and Augustine quickly. The thought of being alone, without a person, frightened me.

Right, left, right, left, right, left ...
Step after step after step after step ...

What felt like hours to me in descending stairs and probably a few miles now had resulted in nothing. I couldn't see a thing, and my feet were numb. I would know if I had reached them. It's not easy to miss Ralloy even in the dark, even though he's avoiding me.

Step ... Step ... my heavy, tired feet went on. But then I stopped. Because I needed the rest. But also because I heard Ruofen's voice.

"RALLOY!" Ruofen's distinct voice echoed. Hearing him gave me a little hope that he actually was down there, and that was reassuring. Well, as much reassurance as that fact can give.

The stairs were too steep to run down, or I would risk falling and getting bruised or broken bones. After resting a little more, I began stepping quickly and lightly, continuing down the stairs.

As I descended, I heard more echoes of "RALLOY!" below. I picked up my pace carefully when I heard the echoes.

And then the stair that I was standing on to rest gave away to nothing beneath. Immediately, I began running down the remaining stairs, my heart beating rapidly regardless of the risk. I heard the stairs behind me crumble, and it spurred me forward, in fear of falling.

Then the crumbling stopped.

I kept on running just to make sure but soon slowed and paused. After a moment, my breathing slowed down.

A minute had passed before I dared to turn and see what had resulted in the stairs crumbling. I was too far down to see what had caused it, and there wasn't any light to see with anyway.

So I slowly stepped up the stairs until I was on level ground.

Level ground? That made no sense, as I had spent the past hour or so descending flights and flights of stairs. I couldn't have reached the top already. It was impossible. There would be light up there.

So much for returning the way I came.

I sat down, weary from all the thoughts spinning in my head and confusing me. I was beginning to have second thoughts about following Ralloy. I had forgotten to bring a communication transmitter. I had no light. And I was getting thirsty.

I pulled my knees up to my chest and hugged them. The events of earlier had begun to take their toll on me, and sleep came swiftly after I muttered, "Help me, God."

Chapter 4

Reached and Realizing

"HELLO? WAKE UP, PLEASE. PLEASE?"

My eyes fluttered open. The person had a sweet voice. As my eyes went into focus, I noticed the lady had fiery red hair. Then I saw her eyes were a steely gray, but fine lines of light blue crossed them. Her face was angular, and she was looking at me gently.

"You're awake now," she half exclaimed, half stated. By now I was, and was wondering how I could see her without a light.

Then I realized there actually was a light. The lady was holding what looked like a cross between a torch and a pole. It was segmented, as if it could collapse in on itself. The top, which held the flame, reminded me of a small satellite dish, and it also was segmented. The flame itself cast a gentle light, so I could see.

"I'm awake," I said while yawning and stretching. The lady stepped back and helped me to my feet.

"Who are you?" I asked as I examined her uniform. It was entirely red, with her tights, knee-length skirt, and long-sleeved shirt. Her clothing seemed out of place for a mountain. *Especially* the Border Mount.

But her two scabbards with hilts poking out were completely appropriate for the hostile terrain of Mount Thias.

"I'm Enstar. And you?" Enstar answered.

"My name is Ceriphina," I said before Enstar's name clicked.

Enstar Lyre was Ralloy's cousin on his dad's side and Ruofen's niece. That explained the hair, and she was also a skilled AttackShift pilot in Caredest's military. And apparently, a swordmaiden as well.

I realize that Mount Thias itself is a soon-to-be battlefield, but why would an AttackShift pilot be this far underground? AttackShift aircraft are built to fly. Besides, an AttackShift aircraft wouldn't fit in this tunnel.

I must have been staring, because she gave me a look that clearly said, "What? People can choose to walk down hundreds of stairs if they want to."

At least, that's how I saw it.

"So what are you doing all the way down here? This isn't a place for kids," Enstar asked.

I proceeded to tell Enstar everything. I could trust Ralloy's cousin. Seven years ago, he had trusted me too. But it had been clear to me that November 1, that had ended. Ralloy didn't seem to trust anyone anymore.

A moment passed after I finished my explanation. "Fair enough," Enstar said, putting a hand on her waist. "Did you notice the door?" She pointed at the right.

I looked, and there it was. The door appeared to be made of solid steel, maybe cybersteel, and there was no disguising it as a stone wall or anything. Maybe no one thought that it would be necessary since it had been hidden under very unstable stairs. It was arched, and it was covered in large grooves. In the middle, split by the air gap, was a capital *B*, and it reminded me of the engraving on the guard's sword.

Then the Barnillon must have really made their home down here.

But what was with the crumbling stairs?

"You want to open it?" Enstar asked me. I shrugged. "Well, if you don't mind, I'll open it." She unsheathed one of her swords and walked the short distance to the door. Then she prodded it with her sword.

After a while, the door slowly creaked open. It appeared as if it hadn't been used in a long time, if not ever.

Enstar pushed on one of the doors, then the other, trying to help the process along.

The doors revealed a small, empty closetlike room that appeared to lead nowhere.

"Seriously?" I said in disappointment. "Who puts a steel door to protect a closet that nobody's even using?" I asked even though I knew I wasn't going to get an answer.

Enstar stepped into the closet. "I really don't know. Unless it isn't a closet," she answered.

"How is this *not* supposed to be a closet?" I asked as I walked in after Enstar.

"What kind of closet has *elevator buttons*?" The pilot pointed to the elevator buttons that were on the left wall of the room.

"Huh," I said after staring for a minute or two. "How did I *not* see that?"

"Maybe because you were so determined that it was a closet," Enstar said playfully.

Note to self: don't jump to conclusions, I thought as I felt a twinge of shame.

"So it's an elevator?" I inquired.

"Well, there's not any indication that it's anything else."
She shrugged. "Besides, what else has elevator buttons?"

She must have noticed me trying to come up with
something and added, "That works?"

I got nothing.

Enstar began examining the buttons. "It looks like 'up'
is not an option, so …?" she trailed off and let me decide. I
didn't want to sit and do nothing, and the thought of more
stairs to descend or ascend really wasn't that appealing.

"Let's go down," I said.

Enstar pressed the down arrow on a button. The elevator
began descending, slowly at first, but then it speeded up and
coasted roughly. It screeched and squealed in protest, so it's
old, as far as I can see. And hear.

"How often do you talk to military commanders,
Ceriphina?" Enstar asked me as we descended.

"I talk to Ruofen more than I talk to Ralloy," I said.
"But more recently, it's Emayne I see at the front door."

Enstar laughed. "Yeah, I suppose you would be used to
talking to military commanders. It's just that most people are …
well, more … nervous around soldiers. You know," she told me.

Because of the threat of Alsekan conquest, many people
were worried that soldiers could be Alsekan spies or infiltrators.
I never figured out how they made the connection. I wouldn't
believe it, as the general of Caredest's army lived across the
street and my adopted brother was a soldier himself. But as
a result, new laws made travel between the mega-nation and
Caredest very difficult, similar to the Zerhali lockdown on its
borders. But then again, not very many people actually *want*
to go to the Arctic Circle. Caredest is much more accessible,
but when war erupts, the lockdown would be completely
ignored by Alseka.

"Yeah, I know," I replied. As the silence returned, I noticed that I could see the walls of the elevator shaft speed past us in place of the elevator doors. I wrinkled my nose as I remembered in history class my teacher had taught about those "two-walled elevators" were used during the Age of Conquest when the Oppression was seizing control of an ill-prepared Setlia. That was over three centuries ago.

No wonder it was old and buried under stairs. I'm just surprised that the elevator hadn't rusted yet.

Soon, the elevator slowed and came to a stop. The view we were greeted with was bright, brighter than the torch Enstar held. It took a minute or two for my eyes to adjust to the light.

Wait. Why would there be light underground?

I saw then that the source of the light was from fluorescent lamps spaced on the walls of a pathway, thankfully flat. The walls of the hallway now seemed to be made out of metal, and the floor was stone tile.

I glanced at Enstar. She had both swords out now and was stepping out of the elevator cautiously. A baton was clipped was to the back of Enstar's belt, replacing the torch, it looked like. I followed softly as I knew that warriors were always stealthy when on unfamiliar turf.

Eventually, we came to another door. This one was made of wood and appeared to be less fortified compared to the other door we had encountered. Weird.

Maybe no one expected anyone to go down all those stairs. So nobody bothered to place defenses on the door. Maybe the tunnel that I followed Ralloy, Ruofen, and Augustine through was the back door. Maybe it lead into a dungeon and we were walking right into it.

What if we were walking into a *trap*? I considered for a moment. The thought of getting trapped by the Barnillon sent a shiver down my back.

"Do you think that this could be a trap?" I blurted suddenly. Enstar turned to face me.

"Maybe. But the Barnillon is pretty secretive, so for all I know, we could be waltzing into a ballroom, a secret laboratory, private quarters, or a tennis court. I really have no idea," the AttackShift pilot quipped, trying to cheer me up. She apparently wasn't worried about anyone hearing us.

I smiled. "A tennis court? Really?" I replied.

"What was I supposed to say, disc golf? Field hockey? I'm pretty sure nobody does *swimming* on or inside of a mountain in a potential war zone," Enstar said playfully. I had been holding in a giggle, but since that's kind of hard for me to do, it exploded, and I laughed for a minute straight.

After I regained my breath, Enstar spoke again, "Since I opened the last door, would you do the honors, Ceriphina?" She swept her hands over to the door.

"Uhh … You can go," I said nervously. I wasn't very eager to open doors into the unknown. At least, not yet.

"Don't you want to open it?" Enstar asked me. I shook my head. "Oh," she sighed, then turned to open the door herself.

It opened from the other side, revealing the solemn face of Augustine, Enstar immediately stiffened. I had told her about him and how I thought he had changed, but it was shocking to see him so … suddenly.

"Who's there?" a familiar voice called. Ruofen. "Are there reinforcements?"

He sent for reinforcements?

He could have.

Augustine turned to the room and said, "Were the reinforcements a young lady with fiery hair?" he asked. I'm sure he saw me as blue really wasn't good camouflage, but he didn't mention me. Maybe he could see Ralloy's hostility and thought it better to keep my presence a secret—at least until I walked through the door or vice versa.

Ralloy. Now I was nervous. How did I know that things wouldn't turn out like five weeks ago? What if he ended up ignoring me? Ralloy was so unpredictable, I couldn't even begin guessing. And this began with me wanting Ralloy to acknowledge that I existed. Just that and only that, if I went straight to the heart. I cared about him, but that was what I really wanted.

I looked down at my feet as I realized that I felt afraid, maybe a little vulnerable. I wanted protection but now I wasn't sure from what.

Chapter 5

Exactly Why Did I Come?

AUGUSTINE STEPPED ASIDE TO LET Ruofen see. "Enstar? What a surprise!" he exclaimed as he came over and hugged her. I backed up to the wall, unsure of what to do at this point. A feeling of dread came upon me. *I had anticipated this. But now, it's the opposite.*

Augustine stepped into the corridor. Ruofen let Enstar go and moved aside to make room for the heir-not-to-be. Augustine met my nervous, faltering gaze with one of concern.

Ruofen noticed and turned to face me.

It became so quiet and still to the point I was sure that Ralloy could hear my fast and shallow breaths.

Ruofen was muscular and a skilled warrior, the reason that he was Varnillon's—and Caredest's—general. He was also a gentleman. But the look he was giving me was one of surprise. He didn't know I was following him. He didn't know I would go this far. I had even surprised myself with my determination.

"Why are you here, Ceriphina?" he said quietly, gently shaking his head. It was as if he didn't want to shatter the silence, for reasons unknown.

I looked down. My face grew hot with shame. I knew he expected a straight answer. And in all the excitement and everything, I had forgotten to think about my explanation. And so I was in this really awkward situation.

Saying I wanted Ralloy to stop being angry when he was only a few feet away was definitely not a good idea.

"I wanted to see Ralloy," I answered quietly. Then I looked at Ruofen.

His stern gaze softened. Relief washed over me. Ruofen understood.

Ralloy's father gave a wan smile. "It's not like I can send you back up all those stairs," he said. Then he walked back into the room he walked out of. Enstar followed him. I began to do the same, but a firm yet gentle hand on my shoulder stopped me. I turned around, and I saw the face of Augustine.

"You followed," he said, giving no hint of what he was feeling.

"Well, I was lost. And I wanted someone to guide me," I deflected. Why did Augustine want to talk to me?

The heir-not-to-be was silent for a minute, then spoke. "Why would you want to be with someone who is avoiding you?" he repeated from earlier when we had first met.

If he's repeating the question, he's probably anticipating a better answer than "It's complicated."

"Basically, I wanted Ralloy to calm down and stop hurting us," I responded honestly in a whisper. Augustine wanly smiled. This answer was definitely better than the previous one.

But why did he ask again? Ralloy might or might not have been angry, so it was probably hard to imagine why I still would want to be with him.

But wait. Would I have gone so far if my true intentions had been selfish? Was there something deeper? Likely genuine?

But like Ruofen said, there's no turning back. I've come too far to back out. And going *upstairs* is much more tiring than going *down*, which was more tiring than you would expect.

Augustine walked through the door. I looked through after he quickly veered out of the way of someone who was standing a few feet from the door frame.

I was now looking several feet away at Ralloy.

He was wearing his standard uniform, tawny pants and a red shirt with the symbol of Varnillon, five flames in a flower sequence on it, above his heart. Or it would have been if it wasn't covered with a hastily wrapped bandage, covering Ralloy's upper chest. He must have gotten wounded when he battled the guard, if he did that. His sword lay sheathed in his scabbard attached to his belt. Ralloy's hands were tight fists, and he kept them at his side. His hair, fiery like his father's, brushed his shoulders. Ralloy's face was expressionless, and his steely gray-blue eyes told me nothing.

It was silent between the two of us. I didn't know what to say. Ralloy didn't say anything. It was awkward. And nerve-wracking for me.

Finally, Ralloy broke the silence. "Why did you want to see me?" he said evenly.

"To have a conversation?" I said, heightening the awkward factor.

"Okay … very strange timing." Ralloy drew out his words. This was awkward for him too.

Somehow, that eased my tension, but not enough to actually show.

"What were you doing before I came?" I inquired. Ralloy gestured to the door as he stepped aside to let me see. Then he abruptly turned and entered the room himself, then moved out of sight.

I tentatively stepped forward. My view was unhindered by the other people.

She had a human-like form, but her head was shaped like an oval on its side. Vivid yellow wings were folded loosely on her back, orange on the rim. White impenetrable scales covered her, a stark contrast with the black mask-like mark on her face. A small gray triangle was likely her nose. Her eyes were closed, and a stripe that tapered on the point began on her forehead and went to the back of her head. Her hands were red, and fingers that started at her knuckles were silver-gray. Her feet were similar, red ankles and silver boot-like feet.

And there was a glass case surrounding it on a raised platform. The case was leaning a little. The floor was stone tile, like the hallway, but now the walls and ceiling were clearly made of seamless steel. Cybersteel.

I approached it. I realized that it was a prisoner.

The Barnillon has strange ways of holding prisoners. How many do they have? Why is this prisoner in glass? Couldn't the prisoner just break it and escape? Why didn't it?

I examined the prisoner closely. Where the eyes would have been, I noticed a fine line, hardly noticeable but present, where the eyelids could meet. The prisoner's eyes were closed. I didn't see them open at any point, so it could be asleep.

Or unconscious.

Or sedated.

Or a patient, but the lack of medical tools—the lack of *any* tools—disproves that theory.

I watched the prisoner's chest move up and down, but I could barely see the movement. It was alive, but barely.

I stood up straight. "We should do something," I said.

"We've been discussing how to do that for the past twenty minutes," Augustine answered.

"Why can't we just carefully cut the glass?" I asked.

"Because the prisoner would still be unconscious. And we already tried that," Ruofen answered. "It's not glass," he added after a second.

"Then what is it?" I questioned.

"It looks like an energy barrier," the general responded.

An energy barrier? I never saw one of those before. According to my energetic sciences teacher, they were similar to a Shield, but were more permanent. Usually, they were to keep invaders out or keep someone in. Or in some circumstances, an invisible wall.

But my teacher never taught us how to *break* an energy barrier. Maybe she couldn't find anyone who could demonstrate one.

"How do we break an energy barrier?" I asked, turning around and facing Ruofen, Augustine, Enstar, and Ralloy. I averted my gaze from Ralloy on second thought.

Silence followed my inquiry until Enstar pulled the baton from her belt. She walked toward me, so I moved aside. She looked like she had an idea. It probably involved that baton by the looks of it.

"So ... you have a plan?" Ralloy asked his cousin.

Enstar paused, looked over her left shoulder, and replied, "It's an idea." She faced forward. "A theory, really." Now she was about where I had stood seconds ago. Enstar held the baton at eye level and stepped backward a little. She held it horizontally and lowered it to match the level of the prisoner's chest. Then she slowly placed the baton on an end—the side with the grooves I only noticed now—facing the prisoner.

Then she pressed something, and the panels slid out into a disc, but more like the shape of those short soccer cones. I recognized the shape as that as the torch, but now the stafflike part didn't extend as before.

Why was she using the torch? And why was it made out of metal?

Suddenly, the energy barrier violently rippled, as if a tidal wave had ripped through it. The torch and Enstar,

THE STORM OF ANGER

however, seemed stable. The transparent barrier flashed the color of the fire of the torch. I stepped backward. Why did the fire of the metal torch react with the energy forming the barrier? Did the fire have an energetic property that allowed the reaction? Was that why the torch was made of metal instead of wood?

The energy barrier dissolved into the air, from the top, then disappearing as if it never were. The prisoner was free-standing, but its eyes were still closed.

Enstar backed up, her hands by her sides. The torch was on the floor and reverted back to its baton state. "That worked better than I thought it would," she said, crossing her arms on her chest.

"Can you please explain what just happened?" I asked, still stunned about the disabling of the energy barrier.

"I'm not an energetic scientist, so no, I can't explain. I'm not quite sure what happened myself," the AttackShift pilot confessed. I guessed that these types of things were way out of her league.

Then it was silent. But my head was full of questions.

Like why didn't the men say anything? Why are they quiet? If it were a warrior's instinct, Enstar likely would have let me know.

Then I looked at the prisoner again.

Before, when it was trapped inside the energy barrier, its wings had been loosely folded in, spread a little to keep air flowing, maybe. But now, they were spread out, like it was stretching, as if ready to fly. The prisoner's body language indicated that it was stretching. The wings folded in again, and the prisoner's eyes opened, and for the first time, I could see them.

They were surprisingly blue. Sapphire blue.

I wasn't expecting blue. But I really wasn't expecting anything, now that I think about it.

Those deep blue eyes looked like they could pierce us, but also confused, as if thinking, *Who are they?* Maybe even suspicious, but that went away when the prisoner glanced at me. Soldiers don't usually mean harm if a girl is traveling with them, but Enstar was a warrior herself. The prisoner might have tensed up if I wasn't there.

The thought of the prisoner possibly attacking us was intimidating. The prisoner just might be one of those types whom you don't want to be against.

But we were staring. The prisoner stared back.

This is the second awkward moment I've had in ten minutes.

"Who are you?" the prisoner asked in a definitely female voice. Her voice was laced with a semi-thick accent, but I had no idea where the accent could possibly come from. But it fit her and her frame.

"My name is Ruofen," Ruofen said, assuming leadership over us—leadership that he actually had—by answering first. There was a silence for a minute, then Augustine introduced himself. The prisoner didn't react or ignite a third awkward moment, which might have surprised the heir-not-to-be.

"And you?" The prisoner turned and gestured to me.

As I opened my mouth to reply, Ralloy responded with, "Ceriph."

Ceriph was what Ralloy would call me before the Terrible Raid. Sane too. It was a nickname that people close to me referred to me as, and Ralloy hadn't called me Ceriph in a long time.

But now the prisoner would call me Ceriph.

"Ceriph. Short for Ceriphina?" the prisoner asked me. It suddenly dawned on me that she wasn't moving her jaw. In fact, there was no evidence of a jaw or mouth at all. It was strange, but with her form, it made sense.

And I forgot how easy it was to deprive my real name from my nickname.

I nodded. "And what about you?" I prompted.

The prisoner looked at me for a minute, as if contemplating whether or not to answer my question. She then spoke.

"I had gotten as close as anyone could have to defeating Zaphn late at night. A few times during the battle, Zaphn hesitated to attack. Once, I stopped to observe the reason of his hesitance when he did, and then he struck a mighty blow when I was off guard. That is how I got here."

"And my name is Shyann."

Chapter 6

Mystery of Shyann

I DON'T KNOW IF SHE intended it, but Shyann made it sound intense. It probably was intense for her, battling the very dragon who never lost. But Zaphn also appeared to have a sense of mercy, letting Shyann live (barely, perhaps) and not attacking Augustine and I, even though he clearly knew we were there.

And if Shyann was able to take on Zaphn, she is either brave or reckless. Maybe both.

Shyann suddenly turned to her right. A tremor ran through our room.

"Does the ground usually shake when you're deep inside a mountain?" Augustine asked, his tone bewildered. I backpedaled into the cold, metal wall. The tremor stopped as I regained my bearings. Earthquakes are unnerving for me. And that was the first one I had ever felt.

"This is not my field. I don't know if earthquakes are normal down here or not," Ruofen responded.

"We are underground?" Shyann asked. The question surprised me. But as I looked around, I realized that there was really no way to know that we were underground, with countless tons of solid rock (unless the Barnillon's base is above us, and this is the dungeon, and the dungeon is always below the castle) above us.

The ceiling must be well built. Whoever designed it was a good architect.

"We're underground," Enstar confirmed.

"We have to get out of here," Shyann stated. After concentrating on a certain part on the opposite wall, she asked, "What's above us?"

"Varnillon," Ruofen began but was cut off by a waving motion by Shyann.

"Good. I remember Varnillon. Has Alseka begun the war at last?" Shyann shook her head. "Don't answer now," she said as if reconsidering her question. She now was looking at the floor we were standing on.

Suddenly, we were surrounded by blue. A light blue that was streaming upward. The streams blurred as they went. I reached out to touch one, wondering where they came from, as we began rising fast. In a few seconds, the trip was over. It took a few more seconds to recover from the swift transport. Shyann swooped overhead, then landed several feet in front of us, her back facing us. She turned as she stood up from her landing position. Shyann quickly looked us over, like she was counting us to make sure we were all present. She visibly relaxed when she was done. I glanced around too. Everyone was here.

"What happened?" I asked, looking at our surroundings. We were in the Razorwood grove, just outside the city.

"That was a Pathway. It was a complex one, so I was not sure it would succeed," Shyann answered.

Shyann was *definitely* more than a *little* reckless. What would have happened if the Pathway had failed?

"So what do we do now?" Enstar asked.

"I believe I have some information for the general." Shyann looked at Ruofen.

"What kind of information?" Ruofen asked. If he was surprised that Shyann knew that he was the general of Varnillon's army, it didn't show.

"It is vital information. Concerning ..." Shyann gestured with her wings over to the peak of Mount Thias.

Ruofen looked at Shyann now the way she looked at me earlier before she told us her name. "Okay," he said and stepped forward toward Shyann. "But is there a catch?" he asked. We didn't know if Shyann was for the Liberators or the Oppression. She did battle Zaphn, but Zaphn might have a lot of enemies. He's intimidating and has a high position.

"Why would there be a catch?" Shyann replied. "It's information. And I don't want anything from you."

Ruofen looked at Shyann for another second, then nodded. Whatever information that passed between them was whispered, and Shyann was making fluid movements with her wings. It didn't look like stretching, though. It looked more ... intentional than that.

But what did Shyann mean?

After a minute, Ruofen stepped back calmly. "Come with me," he said and walked toward Varnillon. Ralloy followed suit, then Enstar, then Augustine. As I tailed them, I could hear footsteps behind me. Shyann was coming as well.

She seemed nice, but it was almost impossible to figure out what her intentions were. One was always suspicious of newcomers on the Border Mount.

Shyann was almost a complete mystery.

Chapter 7

Straight Confession

RUOFEN WAS ON THE PHONE when I walked into his house. A cell phone. He was whispering, but at this point, I was hungry, so I didn't really care what he was talking about. It could be private anyway. It seemed like a day ago since I ate breakfast.

The walls in the living room were orange. Three rustic brown couches surrounded a large wooden coffee table, but I knew that it was used for casual meetings. The more serious ones with the other military leaders and government people were held in Ruofen's study, which was upstairs.

Ralloy went upstairs, maybe to his room. I sat on one of the couches, and Enstar did the same. Augustine still stood. He didn't explain, and no one asked. He was persuaded to take a seat by Emayne, who wasn't bothered by either guest. They had been expecting Enstar. Shyann just leaned against the wall in what seemed like a teenager pose. She seemed more than a little awkward with the surroundings and didn't offer a word.

Enstar excused herself to make a call on her transmitter, a circular handheld one. Those ones used the radio waves. It was probably on a frequency that the Oppression couldn't track.

Augustine was sitting on the couch across from me. His legs were together, and his wooden sword was on his lap. He had detached his scabbard from his belt and was pulling a piece of green cloth from it.

I moved over to him. The heir-not-to-be looked at me and gave a wan smile as he spread the cloth on the table.

The cloth was woven and depicted a picture. Augustine was in the center, someone whom I guessed was the crown prince Zinnune was on his right. A young lady, maybe Augustine's sister, wearing a white dress was on his left. Another Zerhali girl was below him, and an older Zerhali man was above him. There were sticks woven into the structure between Augustine and the women in the picture.

Why was that?

"Why are there sticks there?" I said, pointing to them.

Augustine looked at the cloth. For a while, he didn't say anything. I began to worry that I had asked the wrong question. But then he answered.

"This is Sanova, my older sister," he said, pointing to the young lady in in the white dress. Further inspection proved that her hair was straight. Then he moved his finger to the other girl. "Rei. My younger sister," he said, his voice trembling. Rei's hair was surprisingly blond while the rest of the family's hair was either a dark brown or black. She wore a standard parka, unadorned. That surprised me because she was clearly royalty.

"Rei was humble. She often wore clothes like everyone else in Zerhal." Augustine sighed. He seemed to miss her. Where was she?

"First, Sanova disappeared during the *aurora borealis* in December four years ago, a few days after Christmas. Then a year and a half later, Rei went missing under similar circumstances. Both times tore our hearts apart. Zerhal grieved with us," Augustine concluded. Then he drew a stick from his left sleeve.

"And then recently, Father announced the heir." Augustine didn't bother to continue. It was a story I already knew, and it seemed to be painful for him. Someone who wanted to be king wouldn't think their story hurtful. And Augustine didn't impose any titles. He wasn't intimidating. He even seemed to be almost invisible in Shyann's containment room. Just maybe...that Augustine doesn't want to be a leader anymore.

"Why don't you want to be king anymore?" I asked. Augustine turned to me, his eyebrows raised in shock. People probably didn't ask him that question often. Considering how he was in the Razorwood grove, it appeared like he tried his best to *avoid* people. Mostly.

"Well ..." Augustine drew out the single syllable. The stick in his hand trembled. He closed his hand firmly around it, but he still trembled. I heard him take deep breaths, like this was very uncomfortable for him. "Well ... I was facing Zinnune. Face to face, he dared me to challenge him." "I couldn't. I could oppose him from afar, but when looking at him in the eye? Challenge Zinnune to his very face? No. I couldn't and didn't. I threw my sword, the heir's sword, really Zinnune's, not mine, down to the ground."

"And ran." Augustine took a deep breath. "After that, I decided that becoming king wasn't worth it. But the damage has already been done ... and my heart torn a third time. This time, it was I who did it. Sanova and Rei were taken, against their will, I imagine, but I tore my family *willingly.* I wanted power more than anything. But now ... now I see that power was the thing dividing us, so I don't want it anymore. I don't want my family to be any more broken than it is. I want forgiveness. For our family to be whole again. I would give up becoming king for that. But now, Zinnune might not accept that. He wants the same thing, I know that, but ... I'm afraid that he won't forgive me." Augustine sighed and held his head in his hands.

"Are you actually going to stop being angry?" Sane had asked Ralloy five weeks ago. Now, it seemed that Ralloy's answer was *No. I won't.*

There was a subtle element about Ralloy that I couldn't name in that corridor. Now I knew what it was. Bitterness. It didn't show earlier under the awkwardness of the moment. But it was there. Ralloy didn't show it to me, but it was there. And Augustine was afraid that Zinnune would feel the same way to him. A cold war between brothers.

"What had I been thinking? Why did I want to be king? My desire only broke my family even more." The heir-not-to-be wept. He was repentant. But I really couldn't do anything. He didn't do it to me.

Augustine was sorrowful. How could I help?

He needed comfort, I resolved. So I did what I could; I embraced Augustine. I didn't say anything, and neither did he. His chest shuddered as he wept.

No words were spoken, but I knew that Augustine was grateful. He wanted a soft, soothing touch, and I was giving it to him.

I just kept on hugging him. When Augustine seemed to run out of tears, he looked up. I did too, and I saw Ralloy sitting on the opposite couch.

THE STORM OF ANGER

How long had he been there? I thought.

Ralloy's brow was furrowed, but that was the only thing he expressed. Had he heard the whole confession?

He then turned and walked back up the stairs. We watched. I didn't say a word. Neither did Ralloy.

He was good at hiding his emotions behind a straight face. And that was what made Ralloy so hard to interpret, even harder than Shyann.

Chapter 8

Sane

A CHICKEN LUNCH WAS EATEN in silence for me, Augustine, and Ralloy. He came back downstairs when his mom called him. It surprised me that it was only 11:54, because I had been sure my nap down at the stairs lasted more than a couple hours.

Ralloy's brow was still furrowed, as if his anger were agitated coals on a firebed. He still kept his straight face, but it was easy to tell that it wouldn't take much for the fire to spring up again. And I knew that would not be pretty.

Augustine still looked tender from his confession. His fork trembled in his grasp, like the stick did.

I averted my gaze to my plate. What had Augustine been planning to do with that stick? I had an idea, but it wouldn't ease his pain. It would only worsen it.

I looked at Shyann. Since she didn't have any evidence of a mouth, she didn't need to eat, which makes me wonder where she gets her energy. Maybe from the energy field that radiates from Setlia. It kind of makes sense.

Augustine stood up first and went outside. He brought his little tapestry and wooden sword with him. I looked at the floor in search of the stick. It was on the floor, in two pieces, with splinters surrounding them. I exhaled in relief, then picked the pieces up. Augustine might have broken it when he held it tightly in his hand. I placed them in my parka's pocket.

I finished eating, or as much as my stomach would allow, because I had lost my appetite watching Ralloy eat. I stood up and announced that I was full. Then I walked to the door. Augustine was sitting on the snow-covered porch stairs. I stepped over to him, cleared the snow beside him with my foot, then sat next to him.

"Hey," he offered to me. The heir-not-to-be was staring at the snow-covered street, where a few younger kids were starting a snowball fight. One of them, a wide-eyed curly-haired boy in a big blue parka, rain boots and mittens, turned to look at us.

"Look!" he said, pointing at us. "They're sad." The kid ran to us. "Excuse me, but what's the matter?" he said, tugging on Augustine's sleeve. The kid's gaze wandered over to Augustine's sword. His face brightened. "Cool! You have a sword! Can I touch it?" he asked enthusiastically. Augustine solemnly nodded. The kid reached and picked it up easily. "It's not heavy!" the kid exclaimed

The other kids gathered as the kid waved it around. He looked familiar. But I couldn't place him for a minute.

Then he surprised me with a question: "Ceriphina, where's your brother?"

Now I remembered. My brother Sane had made friends with a kid named Rythan. This little kid was Rythan, and he hadn't seen Sane in four weeks. So of course he wanted to know where Sane was.

Not sure how I forgot about him.

But I didn't know where Sane was either.

"You have a brother?" Augustine asked. I nodded.

"Yes, she does! He looks like you, but smaller." Rythan pointed at Augustine. "Where is he?" the kid asked again.

"I don't know," I said quietly.

"How come? Sane's your brother. You should know where he is. Don't you have any messages from him?" Rythan complained. Large words were difficult for him as he was in kindergarten last time I met him.

"One that I'm sure Sane didn't write," I answered Rythan's question.

"What did it say?" he asked.

"I couldn't read it."

"Oh. Why not?"

"For one thing, I think it was in a different language. And the handwriting was terrible," I told him. Rythan laughed at that.

"Okay. But tell me when you find him!" he said then went off gathering snow, maybe to make a snowball.

"What happened to your brother?" Augustine asked me after a minute. The question didn't surprise me much. It had been asked a lot four weeks ago.

"He went missing four weeks ago. I don't know how or why, but there was just a note on his bed. It looked like it was the writer's first time actually writing," I told Augustine. He smiled for real. It was different than his wan smiles. Those were laced with sorrow. This one wasn't.

"You know how I feel, then," Augustine said to me. I nodded.

Sane was adopted, but he could have taken me in, as I was by myself without him. He was like a father to me. We had been friends with Ralloy and Marsara.

That was before the Terrible Raid.

When it happened, everything changed. Marsara disappeared, and Ralloy began avoiding me. Sane had told me that Ralloy was angry at the Barnillon, who had apparently organized the raid as far as we knew. But as the years passed and Ralloy still kept his distance, even from Sane, I began to suspect that his anger had progressed far beyond simply *anger*. It was deeper now. Bitterness.

Five weeks ago was the last time they ever spoke. They had been close friends, but now the divide between them had grown so wide that Ralloy apparently didn't even care that Sane had gone missing.

Or maybe he was feeling the same thing as Augustine. But if he did, it never showed, as far as I was concerned.

"Yeah, I know plenty how you feel," I said quietly.

Chapter 9

Translated

AUGUSTINE ASKED TO SEE THE note that was left on Sane's bed. I said sure, then walked across the street to my home.

"How does Ralloy avoid you so easily if you live right across the street from him?" Augustine asked me when I unlocked the door.

I shrugged. "He's been doing it for years. He's an expert by now." I opened the door and walked in.

"Where are your parents?" Augustine observed. No one else was in the house. Our footsteps echoed and reverberated through the thick, insulated walls.

"They're away," I said.

"Where?" Augustine asked. I shrugged. I really didn't know. But it didn't bother me as much as it probably should have. I rarely saw them. My parents weren't home usually.

We walked upstairs, up to my room. The walls were pink as they had been ever since I was five. Even though I preferred blue now, I liked the way my room was. Soft carpet covered the floor and was much preferred to the snow outside. One wall was entirely covered in photographs. Fake snowflakes hung from the ceiling, also from my younger days. A desk was in the corner, with a computer on it. I walked over to it and opened the computer. Inside was a piece of paper with an unintelligible scrawl covering most of it.

"That *is* bad handwriting," Augustine commented. "But it's still readable. Barely."

"You can read it?" I asked, surprised. It hardly seemed like English, but that could be because of the terrible penmanship.

"Yes. It isn't English, but I can read a lot of different languages. I also speak them as well, some more fluent than others," Augustine told me. "I wanted to see the note to see if I could read and translate it," he explained.

Wow. I did not see that coming.

But the note could contain information about where Sane is!

Augustine scanned the page, murmuring to himself as he went. He looked over it a few times, then asked for a pen and paper. I found some on my bookshelf and gave it to him. He moved my computer to the side, put the note on it, and began a translation of the note.

In a few minutes, he was done. It read like this:

"Will be transported ... Dimen-Setlan ... Realm-Setlan ... To enter Realm ... Gateway of Var ... on ... Are there ... Barshilian ... left?"

"That's what you could make out?" I said.

Augustine nodded. "The handwriting is very hard to read," Augustine noted. "Are there any more articles of interest around?"

"None that I'm aware of," I replied.

Augustine stood up. "May I look?" he inquired.

I paused for a second. I had only met Augustine today. He confessed that he was wrong for wanting the Zerhali throne more than anything. I told him of a recent hurt that was brought up by a kindergartener. He wanted to help me heal my wound. But I had done nothing for him. Almost.

"I haven't done anything for you. Why do you want to help me?" I questioned. Augustine didn't have to help me. He barely even knew me.

Augustine smiled. "You showed me that you cared," he said. I realized now that he often didn't finish his thoughts aloud. He only did that with topics that had shared experience with me, things that I understood. And by this, I knew that he meant the hug I had given him when he confessed.

But that wasn't the only thing he meant. He told me his story of change when I asked, when he could tell that I cared.

"We can look." I replied to Augustine, referring to his earlier request.

As we entered Sane's room, dust that had accumulated swirled. It was surprising, the amount of dust there was in there after only four weeks. The room was simple—a bed and nightstand, bookshelf, empty laundry basket, computer, and a desk.

Augustine went straight for the computer.

Why would he do that?

I followed behind him. Silently, he opened it.

It took a second to load, but the first thing that popped up wasn't the password page. In fact, it didn't look like anything I had ever seen on a computer screen.

The background was an ominous dim purple color, with veins of brighter purple framing it, as if it was the hard drive of a computer. The content was easily distinguished as something I could not read.

"Can you read that?" I asked. Augustine slowly shook his head to the side.

"It's encrypted... I would need a program." Augustine stared at the screen. As I watched as well, the script had begun to decrypt itself. The first part was already done, and read this: "Sane will be taken to Dimen-Setlan, more known as Realm-Setlan. To enter Realm-Setlan, you must Gate of Varnilon enter. Is there but another of the Barshilian race yet?"

The writer misspelled *Varnillon*.

"At least it's more legible," Augustine noted. I nodded in agreement. The grammar could be better, though. "Does it help?"

Setlan is another planet, farther from us in our solar system. But I have heard of space missions that always failed to land on it. I have never heard of Realm-Setlan or anything else in the note for that matter, except Varnillon and Sane.

"Not really," I said.

Then the screen went dark. Cello music played from the computer in a minor key and suspenseful.

Then an electric voice began to emanate from the speaker system. It made the computer and the desk vibrate, but it wasn't making clear words. It really didn't match the cello's harmony. It never exactly matched the cello either.

Then the cello was overmatched by an electric ensemble that actually matched the vocalizations, as if the musician changed his mind on the song.

And finally, the vocalizations stopped, the music softened, and actual words came out, as if it were a song.

But it sounded unlike any song I ever heard. Its intent was not that of a song.

> Echoes fill the place I reside
> A castress built of lies,
> A place void of trust,

Where swords thoroughly rust.
The tension is thick within the air,
As some have hope and some despair,
But the silent fury rages on,
For the Lyre shall release the storm.

Then the music cut off, and the screen with the unfamiliar type appeared again. It retranslated, staying a little longer for me to see the words *be strong* before the computer turned off.

"That is a very complex program," the heir-not-to-be commented after a moment of silence.

"Yeah. Did you understand anything it said?" I prodded Augustine.

"Not exactly. But I do know a little about the Barshilian race."

"Species or contest?" I asked him jokingly.

Augustine laughed. "Species, but I don't know what kind of races they have. If they have any at all."

Now it was my turn to laugh. I never really expected to be trading jokes with the Zerhali heir-not-to-be, but I was enjoying it. So was Augustine. "So what about them?"

"The Barshals are a different species that come from Setlan. We could consider them aliens, but they have many characteristics similar to Setlian species. The recent reports about the surface of Setlan are also jeopardizing the use of the term. The Barshals' primary energy output is fire and not much of other techniques unless necessary. Barshals are mostly covered in short orange fur with a white chest. They have large foxlike ears coming out of red hair. They have a tail. The one I know of wears clothes in an earthen tone and uses a staff as his main weapon," Augustine told me.

"You only know about one?" I asked. That seemed strange. If the Barshals were sending ambassadors to Setlia for whatever reason, they might at least send two.

"Yeah," Augustine said.

Hmm. Interesting. "Where did you hear about them?"

"I heard about them from Lindsair Lyre," Augustine replied.

Lindsair? Ralloy's uncle who never came to visit. A former master general of the Oppression. Called traitor twice for abandoning the Liberators first, then the Oppression more recently. People don't really know his current position, including his brother Ruofen. Lindsair is a man with a complicated backstory.

"So ... did that help anything?" Augustine asked.

"Not exactly. Interesting, though," I commented.

"Okay."

The room was silent. Augustine began examining the computer. When he looked on the side of it, he must have found something, because he pulled it out and laid it on the desk over the papers on it. It was the size and shape of a small button, and it had two glowing blue rings on it, one inside the other. It was made of a dark-gray metal, and I had the impression that it wasn't made of cybersteel, which was strange, because almost everything that needed metal was made of it these days. The blue rings dimmed suddenly.

"This is foreign technology," he stated. Augustine clearly didn't recognize it, or he would have told me what it was called. He didn't.

"Do you think that might have been where the program came from? I'm certain that Sane wasn't taking any classes for highly advanced computer programming," I said to Augustine.

"Yes, you are correct. I just can't figure out how it got here, though. I don't think that Sane's kidnapper would leave a note pointing straight to them, if we knew what it meant," Augustine pointed out.

I get what Augustine means. That wouldn't make sense … unless someone on the other side wanted Sane to be rescued. And that wouldn't make sense unless …

"Whoever took Sane has a traitor in their midst," I said quietly.

I finally went back to my room after looking unsuccessfully for more indicators of where Sane might have been taken to. Augustine went back to Ralloy's house after Ruofen called him on a transmitter he gave him. So I sat at my desk and looked out the window my desk faced. The window faced the street, where I had a good view of Ralloy's house. The kindergarteners and Rythan were gone now, maybe going sledding or something. The street was empty now, and it was snowing lightly. I could still see the imprints in the snow from when Augustine crossed the street, and the tracks left by the children in last night's snow.

I just looked out the window, not with any intentions. I wondered where Shyann was. Although she was mysterious, I would like her to … be there. Was she with Ruofen? Maybe discussing what Shyann told them. Or something else, like the possibility of Alsekan conquest and the precautions in place to prevent it, if possible. They really could be talking about anything, if they were talking at all, but those seemed like the most likely.

I wondered what Ralloy was doing, but I was hesitant to go over and see because of our previous encounter. It was too awkward and tense to go back there. So I stayed. There was nothing to watch on the ground, so I looked to the sky.

There were a few Zyncosiacs flying in the air. They seemed to be dancing or something like that. It was beautiful. They rolled in the air and spun for a few minutes as I watched, and then they flew away. I looked where they used to be for a few more seconds, then I looked to the ground once more.

Now I saw someone there. Wearing a thin dark parka, with the hood back, stood a figure who was looking in my direction, but not straight in the eye. It was hard to tell because of the distance between us. But I could surely tell that the figure's face was orange and could make out what reminded me of a fox's snout. I noticed foxlike ears poking out of hair as red as Ralloy's.

The figure was now looking hard at me directly. Analyzing me, it looked like. I felt a little worried about why. The figure looked like Augustine's description of a Barshal, but there was no staff. So this one must not be the one he had heard of. But why was the Barshal examining me? How did it even know where I was? Or had the Barshal just noticed me looking out the window as it was walking by? But that seemed unlikely ... not in a future war zone. It just didn't make much sense.

So you have gained Shyann's trust? I suppose that is good enough for me.

The Barshal had been looking at me when I heard that. I heard with my ears, but did she speak with her mouth? It was hard to tell from this distance, so I peered closer, pressing my forehead to the glass of my window. The Barshal didn't communicate again, but just kept on analyzing me. After a few minutes, she turned and walked away, an orange foxlike tail waving behind her.

I had never seen the Barshal before, but somehow I could put a name to that analytic face.

Moraiha. That was the Barshal's name.

Chapter 10

About the Torch

SEVERAL DAYS PASSED. VARNILLON NOW bustled with soldiers, called from the capital to help with defense. Why now, I don't know. There had been plenty of warning days before, though they were all false. Ruofen and Governor Milikitea only conversed about it recently the day we rescued Shyann. They talked about it plenty when the Oppression won the Liberators' War eleven years ago. Everyone is anticipating an attack, even still, because Alsekan territory is literally on the other side of the peak of Mount Thias. Hence, the Border Mount. Also a very dangerous place to live, but Varnillon is Caredest's first defense. So here we are, and here we stay.

My house is being used by soldiers for a place to sleep. Not that I mind. It takes away the emptiness, and Enstar cooks pretty well. I've been helping the AttackShift pilot with things around the house. But the people are usually gone most of the day, probably with Ruofen, so Enstar and I went to my room and talked. Today was the seventh of November, the sixth day of this. I sat on my bed, still in my pajamas since it was ten in the morning and the school decided to close temporarily because of the threat of attack. It happens a little often. So I get to stay at home with nothing to do except for talking with Enstar. She was on the chair of my desk, turned to face me.

We had been sitting there for a little while, not entirely sure how to start the conversation.

"So have you seen Augustine lately?" Enstar asked.

"As in conversation or out the window?"

"Either is fine."

"Then no, not really. He's probably not avoiding you or anything, maybe just helping Ruofen."

"That's probably it. I wonder how he's going to help. Is he going to be on the front lines? Or does he not want to handle war right now and help in a different way?"

"I think Augustine would be good company for Ralloy."

"Yeah, except that he looks like he's ready to lash out at just about anyone right now. How was he before?"

"Avoiding me."

"Right."

Silence again.

Enstar reached behind her and pulled something off the back of her belt. As she brought it to her front, it was the baton-torch that Enstar freed Shyann with on the first of the month.

"I'm going to explain the torch now. Is that fine with you, Ceriphina?" Enstar asked me.

"I think that you don't need to ask, but the answer is yes," I replied. Enstar giggled a little.

"Yeah, maybe I didn't need to, but I wanted to clarify," the AttackShift pilot responded. "So the torch. I got it in the mail a while ago. There wasn't any mailing address for who sent it to me, but there was a note inside the package. It pretty much explained everything. It said that my uncle

Lindsair had sent it. The torch itself is one of a few models of an energetic torch that his friend designed … or redesigned, according to the letter. Apparently, it is engineered to not hurt people, however that works. So I think that was how the energetic barrier was broken. You remember?"

"It would be hard to forget." I laughed, remembering all the ripples the breaking of the barrier caused. Enstar laughed too. "But does the fire actually not burn? I mean, well, you know about Lindsair …" I trailed off. Most people don't know what to think of Lindsair. Both of his brothers, Ruofen and Enstar's dad, are in Caredest's military, and Ruofen leads it. But since Lindsair had betrayed them and then the Oppression, people don't really trust him all too much altogether. He's outside of known civilization though, as far as I know. He's never visited, and no one's really seen him at all.

"Well, it's not like I could test it, and it would be strange if I just asked the first person I saw to stick a finger into a fire that may or may not be harmful. So do you want to test it, Ceriphina?" Enstar asked me.

"Uh …" Test it myself? It would be impressive if the theory was true, but it would be painful if it wasn't. But I would never know if I didn't try. "Okay …"

The torch activated, lengthening to its full height of four feet. Enstar stood to keep her grip on it, and after a second, it lowered down so the flame was at my eye level. The fire was orange and looked semitransparent. It appeared to solidify for a moment, look like real fire, and then returned to its original state.

I slowly reached my hand close to the fire. The fire didn't feel hot. Warm, but not uncomfortably so. If it was just warm, then the fire probably couldn't *burn*. So I reached closer.

I closed my eyes and cringed as my hand entered the fire.

There was no burn, just warmth. I opened my eyes in shock as I withdrew my hand and stared at it. There was no mark that I had ever put it in the fire. And it was warm, like the fire.

"Whoa …"

"That means that the fire really is engineered to not harm people," Enstar concluded.

"Yeah … I guess so," I replied.

Chapter 11

Symbolic Dream

It was night now, and I was in bed. It was no small feat to finally go to sleep, considering my brain was still trying to comprehend the fact that non-burning fire existed, but I finally managed to do it. I drifted into slumber quietly.

I felt like I was in microgravity or in water, but I could breathe easily. As I looked around, I saw that I was surrounded by white, except for something I saw to my right. I turned to see the object. It was a statue of a young warrior with a sword drawn. The details on the clothes was apparent and extremely precise all the way down to the symbol of Varnillon on the chest of the uniform the warrior wore. There was a stark difference between the body and the face, as the face had absolutely no detail. There was hair on the head but no facial features.

Then as I watched, a small arrow came from nowhere and hit the statue's abdomen. The arrow was small and reminded me of a porcupine's quill. The statue recoiled, as if it were animated by cybersteel or something.

Then swiftly came another arrow. This one was larger, like an actual sized arrow, and it penetrated the statue's chest, right below the five-flame symbol of Varnillon. The statue was blown back by the force of the blow, responding like a person. But I noticed that it didn't utter a sound. The wounds would have been painful for a human, but the statue was suffering in silence, if the statue could be in pain. Could it?

Then an even larger arrow, big enough to be a javelin, streaked through the air. As it passed, I saw that it had six extensions of the arrowpoint.

The third arrow pierced the chest of the statue, right at the center of the symbol, where the heart would be. But the statue stood still, unmoving, as if oblivious to the pain at this point.

But no, not oblivious—hiding the pain, which is strange for a statue, but that was what it looked like.

Suddenly, the quill arrow disintegrated. Turned into dust and blew away as if it never existed. The second arrow did the same, only not as fast as the first one. But the third— the javelin—stayed.

As I watched, the javelin-arrow slowly went deeper, deeper into the chest of the statue. When it stopped, the arrowhead was completely buried in the stone.

Then lines cut themselves into the chest, in a snowflake pattern, around the embedded javelin-arrow. At first, it was small, barely noticeable, but the design grew swiftly. When it covered the statue's chest, the lines began to glow red. The lines were filled in mere seconds, and the engraving continued at an even faster rate. In a minute, the entire statue was covered in the red lines, even its face.

The statue suddenly tensed. Fine white lines suddenly covered it.

I suddenly was thrust into darkness as I heard an explosion (or could it have been an implosion?) and a long, loud, heart-wrenching cry.

Suddenly, I saw a familiar face—Ralloy's. He looked stern. And I realized and remembered that the uniform on the statue was his.

Chapter 12

Military Summons

I HAD WOKEN UP GROGGILY. I was surprised that I didn't wake in the middle of the night in a cold sweat. I was looking out the window again, but Enstar was absent. The house was also quiet, a luxury that had eluded the house for the past few days. I took it in for a minute, then began to wonder where all the soldiers had gone.

Suddenly, my computer emitted a chirpy sound. I opened it, entered the password, and checked my messages. At the top of the list was a message from a frequency I hadn't reached in a while—Ruofen's. Curiously, I opened the message, knowing it could be important.

The message read, "Ceriphina, please come to the general's tent on the Varnillon border camp. I would like to talk to you as soon as possible about something very important."

This is Ruofen's gentle commanding style. Basically, if he wants to see me, I'm probably going to go.

And go I will, so I need to put on warmer clothes and change from my pajamas.

The outskirts were rocky, but small red flags along the way helped, especially in the snow. The gathered soldiers were in small tents that they brought with them. Various AttackShift vehicles were hovering several feet in the air. One looked like one of the newest models, that could shift to work on the ground instead of only in the air. Very useful for crashes.

Ruofen's tent was easy to spot; the general's shelter was forest green and had the flag of Varnillon flapping in the wind above it. I navigated my way through the maze of tents and walked into the forest green one.

The flap opposite the one I entered was just closing as I stepped in. Inside the tent was Ruofen, already in his armor, and Augustine.

The heir-not-to-be was outfitted in armor as well, and it gave him an air of authority. Before, he just appeared to be a roaming mercenary with no intent whatsoever. But now, Augustine really looked like a warrior. A skilled one too, one that no one would dare cross. A real sword hilt stuck out of his scabbard, and that only added to the effect. The symbol of Varnillon embedded in the chest armor was relieving.

Both men visibly relaxed as I entered the tent. It must have been tense with Ralloy in the room, especially with this topic.

"Ceriphina, I'm glad you came." Ruofen sighed. "Augustine and I have decided to let Ralloy go on a mission. He will go onto enemy territory, but he will *not* go alone." He placed special emphasis on *not*. The general turned to Augustine. He pointed to him. "Augustine, you will go and act as Ralloy's guardian. If necessary, be a wall between him and the Barnillon. You can do that, right? Be a wall?" Augustine nodded. "Good. Just in case Ralloy does anything crazy."

Then he turned to me and sighed. "This is the first time I'm doing this, but it may end up saving Ralloy's life, if it comes to that."

Ruofen looked at me in the eye. "I want you to go with Augustine and Ralloy. I know Ralloy might not listen to you in an ordinary circumstance, but the battlefield is not an ordinary circumstance. If faced in a life-or-death situation, he just might listen to you," Ruofen told me.

Ralloy might listen to me if he wasn't doing anything crazy. But that wasn't guaranteed. Would he listen to reason when he was angry and bitter? Maybe not. I felt nervous and kind of scared to think about what could happen to Ralloy.

I'm scared to go, but I can't afford not to go, not if it costs a life.

"I'm afraid," I told Ruofen.

The general smiled. "I don't know a lot of young ladies like you, Ceriphina. You are very honest."

I felt warm when he said that.

"I believe that you *need* to go with Ralloy. He may not think so, but it may be essential that you go," Ruofen said solemnly to me. He put a hand on my shoulder. "I trust you," he whispered.

I thought about it.

Then I whispered back, "Yes, sir."

Chapter 13

Abilities and Gifts

WE WERE FOLLOWING RALLOY AROUND the Razorwood grove. Since his father was allowing him to choose the trajectory of his assignment (which in my opinion was very dangerous), he had decided that the first step was to locate a larger entrance into Mount Thias and see exactly how much there was to the Barnillon's base. But that was all he told us, so he could be planning something dangerous or risky. I don't know, but with Ralloy, it was wise to expect the unexpected.

Of course, that also meant that there was a small possibility that he hadn't planned very far into this mission and was taking things one step at a time, which would be a bad idea for a leader.

We snuck around the trees until Ralloy signaled us to stop. He ducked down, and so did we.

I peeked around his shoulder. Ruofen had given me armor, but it hardly felt like it. It was so easy to move in it. It looked like regular snow clothes and was even blue.

At first, I saw nothing in the snow and brambly trees ahead. There was a lump of strangely shaped snow in the middle, but that was all.

Then the "lump" moved. It jumped into the sky, and came down looking like Shyann.

I stared. I think we all stared in surprise.

She looked at us like she knew we were there even though none of us made a peep. She also seemed to say, *What's so strange? I do this all the time. Pretty much.*

Or was that me?

It's the Snowblind Effect.

I was definitely hearing something. With my ears. Not my head. But it looked like I was the only one who could hear Shyann. But it was hard to tell because of her lack of a mouth.

Then Ralloy sprang forward, drew his sword, and dashed toward her.

My mind reeled as he readied his sword to strike her.

Shyann blocked the blow with her arm and pushed his blade away. She didn't retaliate. There was no mark where the blade hit her.

Ralloy tried again, this time aiming for Shyann's abdomen. She stepped back, avoiding the hit, and again did nothing in return.

I stood up. Augustine did too. "Didn't Ruofen tell you to be a wall for Ralloy?" I asked him.

"He specified the Barnillon. I doubt that Shyann is part of their group," Augustine responded.

Ralloy attacked. Shyann blocked. Ralloy feinted an attack, then went in. Shyann didn't fall for it, jumped into the air above him, somersaulted in the air, and landed several feet behind him. Ralloy spun around and charged toward her.

Who ARE you? I heard. This time it was clearly Ralloy. But he had been silent this whole time. Shyann didn't react, which meant that she couldn't hear him, or she was as good as Ralloy at hiding her feelings. Which could make sense.

Shyann moved to the side, and Ralloy almost ran into a tree. He leaned against it, just breathing for a minute.

Then he stepped back a few feet, farther than his sword reached.

And he swung at the tree.

I saw for a fact that his sword did not even scrape the tree's bark. There was a good three inches in between them.

Yet the tree began to fall.

When it was almost level with the ground, it disappeared.

And reappeared, stripped of its branches, several feet above Shyann.

She stared at it for a second, then made a slashing motion at it. The log split in two, and the halves landed in the snow beside her. Then Shyann looked at Ralloy as if saying, *How did you do that?*

Augustine placed a hand on my shoulder. He was trembling, and a look said that his face was lighter than normal. "How long has he been able to do that?" he asked me in a quiet voice.

I was shocked as well. But Sane had told me that sometimes Ralloy had intentionally missed targets by a little bit, but they still ended up cut. Sane thought that Ralloy had figured out how to manipulate the energy field. But that wasn't possible for a human—at least, according to the science we had been taught. But my science teacher had told us about a recently discovered dimensional thing that apparently changed all the rules about the energetic sciences. I forgot what it's called, but Ralloy appeared to be using it to his advantage.

Unless this is some Lyre trait that I never heard of and never saw in action before.

"Maybe a couple of, umm, seasons? Six to seven months?" I tried to answer. That was that first time I had heard of these occurrences.

Ralloy and Shyann were now locked in a heated staring contest.

Who are *you, Shyann? And what else do you know?* I heard from Ralloy. I began feeling a heat sense emanate from him. Barely visible arcs of orange clustered at the hilt of his sword around his hand. A few streaked across the blade past the hilt and looked as if they were fire.

That was a first. Never before had I seen Ralloy's sword—or any blade for that matter—do that. It had to be energy. Visible energy. What the question was, was it intentional or not?

Shyann glanced at Ralloy's blade, though. She was just as surprised as anyone here. *A blade extension and an invisible Pathway?*

Now I know *what* he did, but I feel like no one is going to have an explanation. And Ralloy may not be open to discussion at the moment.

Then Ralloy swung his sword again, probably aiming for Shyann's neck area, if she was closer. But this time, she blocked with her left hand; Ralloy's attack was to her right. Maybe the blade extension again. Ralloy had apparently mastered more than a few inches.

Shyann twisted her hand, dropping it to her side. Ralloy finally seemed to relax, sheathing his sword. They looked at each other, just breathing for a minute or two.

"You attacked because you were suspicious of me, correct?" Shyann asked the young warrior.

Ralloy kept his glare for a few seconds before nodding. He remained silent.

"Because I risked a Pathway that could have failed."

Another nod.

"It didn't fail."

Nothing. This was a statement.

Finally, Ralloy spoke. "Why didn't you attack back?" he asked.

"I may be reckless, but I am not ruthless. I could have done much damage, but I didn't. You are not a threat to me." *At least, not yet.*

Ralloy now took deep breaths. He remained silent but now walked on the way we had been going at first before we encountered Shyann. We stepped out from the trees. Augustine went over to Shyann. I followed and barely heard Augustine say softly to her, "I think it would be wise if you come with us."

Shyann nodded. "I think it would be best too," she replied.

Augustine appeared satisfied with her answer and followed Ralloy. I walked up to Shyann. "Were you talking to me when Ralloy was attacking you? And no one else could hear except for me?"

She waited a minute after the others were a short distance away before replying. "Yes. I was speaking to you. I am not aware of how, though. It came ..." She paused, thinking. "Naturally, I suppose. It just came," she said plainly. Shyann looked pensive when she said it, though, as if it wasn't true, and she knew it.

She waited a little more, then spoke again, but quieter. "It was intentional, and because I gave you an energy trace. With it, I know where you are, and anyone who can feel energy signals knows where you are." I immediately thought of Zaphn when she said that and shuddered. He probably felt plenty, but I wasn't exactly threatening to an Exposial dragon. Shyann, however, could put up a fight. "I believe that the trace may have enhanced previous hearing abilities. I noticed, and used them to communicate with you only." Shyann explained again. This time, it sounded like the truth. I wondered why she lied the first time, but I had another question.

"Previous abilities?" I asked. "What previous abilities?"

Shyann shrugged. "How would I know? They are yours, not mine. If anything, I would have expected an explanation from you," she said, then walked off after Augustine and Ralloy.

I followed after them, with a few questions in mind. Did Sane know about the abilities that Shyann said I had? Was Shyann even telling the truth? My brain felt ready to explode.

And there was still the Ralloy problems. I sighed. I was ready to take a nap, but here was the last place I would want to sleep. I could freeze, and a glance at the sky told me that the overhead clouds were laden with snow. A few flakes were coming down already.

As I caught up with everyone else, one of the snowflakes drifted in front of me.

It was orange, the same orange the arcs on Ralloy's sword had been.

That was shocking. I had never seen orange snow before. As I walked on and saw more flakes like that orange one, I began to wonder if there was a connection.

But to what?

Chapter 14

In for a Surprise

We quickly found a larger tunnel in the mountain's side. We went inside, following Ralloy into a sharp turn. The tunnel was flat and dark. Light from two torches was visible up ahead, with a large arched double door in between them.

The door was heavily decorated, with the symbol of Zerhal dominating it. The doors were ajar, so Ralloy slipped through them. Augustine followed, then I, then Shyann.

It was a dim, little-lit interior. The walls extended much farther than the door. There were pillars placed closely together lining the extensive hallway.

I didn't get the chance to see more as Augustine grabbed my wrist and pulled me between a column and the wall.

Augustine pulled me close to him. He did the same with Shyann and Ralloy. We were all in a huddle now.

"Why does the Barnillon's castress look very, very, *very* similar to the Norheil castress?" Augustine asked in a hushed whisper. He was certainly shocked.

"We don't know!" Ralloy whispered intently. "I saw the exact same part you did! I never saw the actual *thing* before today!"

Same here (does an elevator count?). I don't think Shyann would give much information. Not to mention, this should be a replication, not the real Norheil castress.

Augustine seemed to have given up asking.

"Okay, okay. Follow me. If this castress is a replica, I should know my way around." The heir-not-to-be sighed. Then he stepped out from the pillars. Ralloy went after him, then I did. I listened for the warriors' footsteps, how fast they were. They were hurrying, so I did the same.

We started up stairs. They leveled off quickly (thankfully), and we continued in a hallway.

"Augustine? Exactly where are we going?" Ralloy asked. Augustine's footsteps continued.

"A room," he said simply as he went on. Augustine seemed to not want to specify since I doubt that anyone in our company actually knows which room he means.

We continued to walk for several minutes until Augustine stopped. There was a light ahead of us around a corner. Augustine tiptoed to the bend and stopped again there. We followed him.

I saw a double door with two torches on either side. The door was arched, like the castress's main entrance. This one was made of wood, however, and had an engraving of an uppercase *B*. This was fancier than the crude etchings on the guard's sword or the old elevator door. There was a pillar of stone with a dancer's long ribbon wrapped around it, forming a *B*.

A dancer's ribbon? Usually, girls are interested in dancing (I might be an exception because I have other concerns). *So whoever is in that room is probably a girl. I seriously hope Ralloy's chivalry sense will interfere with his anger toward the Barnillon.*

79

Augustine placed a firm hand on the young warrior's shoulder. Then he stepped forward to the door and knocked.

The sound reverberated through the air, surprising me. Why did he knock? Surely whoever was in there knew we were here now.

Why did you do that? Now they know we're here! I heard from Ralloy. I felt his heat simmering, like he was getting ready to attack someone. Not a happy feeling.

The right door opened a crack inward. "Who's there? Are you friend or foe?" a female voice asked. She appeared to be scared.

I don't know if we are either at the moment. But her voice … I feel like I've heard it before. I just forgot from where and when.

"We are …" Augustine began. He evidently had no idea. Ralloy would certainly be against anyone in the Barnillon, but Augustine? I felt like it was impossible for him to be angry after all that he has been through. He would appeal to be compassionate toward the girl. I would go with Augustine, and Shyann … might.

The door began to close, and Augustine let go of Ralloy's shoulder and reached out to the door. "Wait! I mean, no one in my company will harm a girl," he said. Ralloy cast him an annoyed look that either meant *I'm supposed to be leading* or *She's clearly part of the Barnillon. Are you seriously going to let her go? Do you realize what they did to me?*

Probably the latter one.

"H-how many are there?" the girl whimpered.

"Four. One is not a warrior," Augustine stated without hesitation. I looked behind me. Shyann stood there, completely fine. She was complying with the heir-not-to-be, but Ralloy didn't seem to be so ready to obey. His fists were clenched and stiffly against his thighs.

"All right," the girl said. In a second, the right door continued opening. A tall girl jumped out, grabbed Augustine's hand, and pulled him and Ralloy though the door. Then she repeated that with me and Shyann.

Ralloy had his hand on the hilt of his sword. Augustine held him back with a hand directly over his heart. I whirled around to face the girl. Who was she?

She quickly closed the door and locked it faster than I would have expected. Then she faced us.

She was indeed tall, almost Augustine's height. Her face was angular. Grayish-brown eyes examined me. Brown hair fell down to her waist in a ponytail high on her head. She was wearing a lavender shirt with see-through loose sleeves. Her legs were covered by shorts that went down to her knees. Her feet were bare.

I seriously doubt that the girl would be able to survive the low temperatures outside. Or if she was aware that it was snowing outside.

"I think you can stop it." She smiled, then walked over to a desk with a computer on it. The girl tapped some keys, then turned to us.

"I'm Masseran. May I have the pleasure of your names?" she asked.

Augustine didn't seem so ready to introduce himself. Ralloy actually wasn't looking angry and was staring in surprise. Shyann was silent for whatever reason.

So I stuck out my hand and said, "My name is Ceriphina." Masseran shook my hand gingerly.

"And ... ?" She looked at the rest of us.

"Shyann," Shyann said.

"I-I'm Ralloy," he stuttered. That was a first. I never expected him to stutter inside the Barnillon's castress.

"I … am Augustine." The heir-not-to-be immediately cringed, awaiting the realization.

That evidently never came.

"I've heard of people who loved the sound of their own name, but someone who cringes when telling their name? Now, that's a first." Masseran laughed.

Augustine relaxed. "It's … I just thought that you would bring up a very uncomfortable topic for me. It's happened before," Augustine explained.

"If it's related to the news, it would be a miracle if I managed to get some. Unless you count countless math equations." Masseran sat down in a chair and picked up a cello that was next to it. "Seriously, I've been here for a year, and I don't even know if King Bengial decided on king or president at the moment. And that's like basic knowledge in Caredest! It's either math or cello sheet music. And food and water. And I haven't gotten either in the last month or two! Seriously, I've mastered the last ten pieces those people gave me. I'm ready for something more challenging!" Masseran sighed, exasperated, then picked up a cello bow from the ground. She began playing softly. "I am so glad that you guys are here. I need someone the talk to. I mean, I would talk to Zaphn if he would listen. But he probably won't. He's only been here once. And for no real reason. It would have actually been enjoyable and less intimidating if he interacted! Depending on what he said. He just stood there or whatever, listening to my cello practice. Then he left. I've heard as him as a fierce warrior dragon, so it was strange to see him not in action. Maybe he secretly has a passion for cello music. But if he did, he would be here more than once. It's weird. Even though I can do calculus in the tenth grade, I can't figure out Zaphn!" Masseran exclaimed.

"Yes, he is very hard to figure out," Augustine said. I nodded, then sat on the floor.

"Oh, you can sit on the bed," she said. I went and sat next to her.

"So ... What did you want us to stop?" Shyann managed to interject.

"Ooh, right! The storm of anger, technically why I was doing all those equations. Not that I wanted to. This place is a maze, and even though the door is unlocked, it's all I can do to not to get lost. I don't think the cello has to do anything with it, but the equations were being used by a scientist I met on one of my excursions. He seemed really desperate to get out, like me, but he said that I had more freedom than him. He couldn't leave the laboratory he was in. He couldn't even get through the door I came through, like an invisible wall was holding him back. It was strange, but it was sad to watch. Then he decided to tell me what he knew about the storm."

"He knew pretty much everything about it since he designed it. He said his name was Alexion, by the way. Alexion said that he was also being forced to work on the storm of anger, and wanted to stop it. He had more contact with Zaphn, but they were pretty much enemies, which isn't surprising. Zaphn has a lot of enemies. But he never said who was forcing him. I didn't ask." Masseran stopped playing her cello.

"About the storm?" Shyann asked, a little wearily. Masseran was very talkative. But that's probably to be expected in her circumstance.

"Okay, let's see what I remember," she said.

A few minutes passed by before she began talking again. "The storm of anger was previously impossible. There is something, though, that changed the rules. I have no clue on what it's called. The storm is comprised of energy and energetic anger. However I don't know where the anger part would come from …" Masseran trailed off.

And the Lyre shall release the storm. Whoever wrote that strange poem must have known about the storm of anger. And the only Lyre I knew who was ready to explode was Ralloy.

We have trouble. Ruofen was right when he said that the battlefield is not an ordinary circumstance. I've never been on one, and this one could be the most complex one ever. Why didn't Ruofen send someone with more experience?

Maybe because he knew that nothing could prepare any soldier for this. I don't think anyone could not be knocked of their feet if they hear that they have to fight a man-made storm made up of anger. It sounds impossible, but I felt like Masseran wouldn't lie to us. Not to the first real human company in a year.

Except for Shyann. She isn't human.

Which is a little … unusual.

Masseran doesn't seem bothered by it.

"The storm of anger is also very dangerous, which could be the entire point. Alexion said that the storm was meant to spur on the second Liberators' War. Not that he wanted to. He never said it, but I think that he's secretly a Liberator himself, but why would he hide it? Maybe because of Zaphn," Masseran finished.

Liberators' War II could be catastrophic. The first one was, and the Liberators *lost* the first one. They were defeated eleven years ago, after three hundred years of fighting. We were preparing for an invasion from the Oppression, but not another Liberators' War. Since we were in the closest proximity to Alseka, Varnillon and the Border Mount would be hit the hardest.

And to attach Ralloy to it? That could be a plan to draw Lindsair, Ralloy's uncle, out of hiding. For the Oppression, he's public enemy number one. He used to be one of the best generals they had, but he disappeared a year ago. Ruofen believes that he returned to the Liberators and didn't establish contact yet. Since the Lyre family was in the Liberators for generations, he earned the nickname of "traitor twice."

Basically, this is already complicated. And this is just in my head.

"Of course." Shyann said. Augustine nodded in agreement. Ralloy … I don't even know what he's feeling right now.

"So I think you can stop the storm of anger." Masseran added.

Is she being sarcastic or serious? This feels like one of those barely interoperable teenager moments.

We stared for a moment. Even Shyann seemed doubtful of that statement. She maybe could stop it, but a storm is very … hard to fight.

"What makes you think we can stop a storm that was previously physically impossible?" Augustine asked.

"I know so." Masseran grinned. "And I'm coming too! I'm going to get out of here!" She jumped off her chair. Then she sat again, like she remembered something important. "Alexion too. We have to get him out of that laboratory!" she exclaimed. Then she got up again and began pacing.

"Not the direction I expected this mission to go," I heard Ralloy say under his breath.

I don't think anyone here anticipated this. But it's not like we can stop it. And there's still the storm of anger to deal with.

I sighed. My brain needed a break, and it felt like this had barely begun!

Chapter 15

Reencounter

WE WERE FOLLOWING MASSERAN AND the cello that she had decided to bring along down an air duct that was big for an air duct. I could walk upright in it. The air was also warmer than what I would have expected in an air duct. Masseran said that the guard had doubled a month ago, so this was probably the safest route, aside from the fragile metal the air duct was made of, which was surprising since Masseran said that the castress was made with cybersteel. You would think that the air ducts would be stronger, but apparently, they weren't.

As I walked, I suddenly heard a faint roar. I stopped walking in shock. Shyann stopped by my side. "Did you hear something?" she asked me. I nodded. "What?" she asked softly.

"A roar. A faint one," I replied.

I stiffened as I heard a voice. *Argh! Who ... what am I ... fighting? Show ... show yourself!*

"Who's that?" I asked. No one here was battling an invisible foe that he couldn't identify. And I haven't heard this voice before ever.

"Who's who? Did you hear someone?" Shyann asked. I nodded again. Another roar echoed, this time stronger. I continued walking, faster than before. This was unnerving! Who was that?

Another roar sent me running. Then I heard a *No* ...

And the floor began cracking under my feet. I ran faster, trying to outrun the falling floor. I saw the others ahead. *I just need to catch up.*

"Ceriph! Stop running!" I heard Shyann yell.

But my foot landed on glass at that moment, and I fell through a skylight in the air duct.

"Aaaaahhh!" I shouted. I was falling down to a stone tile floor, with white rectangular tables scattered throughout the room. I saw a man looking up at me, with a lab coat and starkly blue hair. His face was stricken with surprise and fear, but there was a glimmer of hope in his gray eyes.

Then it quickly turned to fear, and he seemed to notice something behind me. I tried to turn around to see, but that was when I struck the ground.

I had landed on my side, but the impact was less painful than I thought it would be.

But then Shyann hit the ground beside me.

She was facing me, and I was close enough to tell that her eyes were closed tightly—in pain. Her chest heaved up and down. She must be injured, but how? And by whom?

Shyann groaned as she lifted a finger and pointed to the air duct I fell from. "Za ... phn ... up," she moaned. I looked up to where she motioned.

I saw an Exposial dragon hovering in the air next to the air duct, with Masseran (still holding her cello), Augustine, and Ralloy in his fists. The air duct had a chunk missing from it—probably obliterated—and was precariously dangling from the ceiling. The ceiling looked like a dragon crashed through it, but the solid rock above it was intact. I couldn't wonder about that, though, because the dragon turned his head to me. A burn scar covered his left cheek and part of his jaw.

Zaphn.

But he was not the Zaphn that had spared Augustine and me when we first met. This Zaphn didn't look like he secretly enjoyed cello music. This Zaphn looked more like the Zaphn on the battlefield. Fierce. Powerful. The enemy.

A roar that reverberated through the large room had me covering my head with my arms. *That's the same roar I heard in the duct!* I realized. But I knew that wasn't entirely right. The voice was the same, but the tone, the message it carried was different. The first two I still couldn't identify, but this one was something like a battle cry.

In my mind's eye, I saw Zaphn descending down to the ground. I sat up and saw the man in a lab coat kneeling over

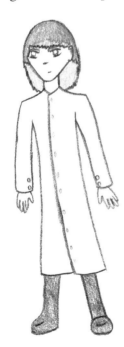

me and Shyann. He backed away from me—no, from Zaphn.

"What is the meaning of this, Zaphn?" the man said in a thick Russian accent.

"You should know very well that it is the eve of the storm, Alexiov." Zaphn growled.

Zaphn was the one who was battling the invisible foe!

Uh-oh. This is going to end badly. An unfamiliar voice said.

"Alexion," the man whispered. "My name is Alexion."

"I also see that your guard was compromised, if Shyann was allowed to escape and come back with company." Zaphn said.

That was the plan. The same voice said plainly. It seemed to be intended for Zaphn.

"You know very well that I am a scientist, not the captain of the guard. It is not my responsibility. Besides, there is not much I can do locked up in here." Alexion motioned to a door at the right.

Zaphn narrowed his eyes. Then he turned to me. "Ceriphina. Why would you come here?" he asked me cryptically. I backed up from him and said nothing. I was scared.

"You don't want me to know, don't you? Or are you scared?" he inched his head closer and closer to me. It was completely obvious that I was afraid of him.

"She is a girl, a child! You cannot harm her!" Alexion shouted. Zaphn stepped backward. I felt Shyann's hand on mine, and she pulled me to my shaking feet. Trembling, she stepped toward the dragon, giving me a view of her back.

I silently gasped. Shyann's right wing was limp, and the mainstay was completely snapped in the middle and hanging down. Blood was coming slowly out of the wound. Shyann must be in so much pain, and she couldn't fly now.

"I will not let you hurt Ceriph," she said in a low tone.

"Shyann. I have defeated you before. And I have already wounded you. Why would you risk your life protecting someone?" Zaphn growled.

"For the same reason as I had seven years ago."

"You failed seven years ago."

"Failure isn't final. I will not give up my values to save my own life. I won't sacrifice Ceriphina!" Shyann exclaimed, making a motion with her unbroken wing to me.

Realization crossed my heart. Shyann and Zaphn were fighting over me. Were they fighting over me seven years ago?

"And again and again, you prove your claims to recklessness. I will not fight you now, but I will tell you something." Zaphn came close to Shyann, almost nose to nose. "Ceriphina, whom you protect so valiantly, is a shield to the eye of the storm. Yet at the same time, she is a stinging arrow in my side, like your broken wing," the dragon whispered.

"Ceriph as a shield, I understand, but as an arrow? She is not a warrior. Why do you think she is afraid? Ceriphina has no warrior training. How can she be a threat to you, Zaphn?" Shyann questioned Zaphn. She was standing her ground, and not giving way. But the question ... was that the best idea in the world?

"Ceriphina is stronger than you think," Zaphn stated. Shyann said nothing aloud to this, but told me, *How so? Do you have more than an exceptional hearing ability?*

I stepped backward. This was getting intense. Getting in between these two in a battle would prove very dangerous.

Suddenly Zaphn pounced upon Shyann. I jumped to the side. The dragon toppled Shyann's smaller frame easily. As she landed on her back and on her wing, she let out a pain-ridden yell. Zaphn placed a forearm firmly upon her chest. Shyann shuddered in pain. Now Zaphn was restricting her air flow, which could be very limited in the first place, because of her lack of a mouth.

Now the Exposial dragon looked fiercely at me in the eye. "I believe that you have gotten the idea, Ceriphina. You are in my way." Zaphn then lifted Shyann up from the ground.

"Don't hurt her!" I managed to squeak softly.

"Ah, so the protected one finally has a voice! Don't worry, she won't die, but I will indeed hurt her!" Zaphn cried then flung Shyann to the wall. The cybersteel crumbled and cracked as if it were stone. Shyann, however, didn't make a sound. All the pain must have knocked her unconscious.

Zaphn now turned his full, undivided attention to me. I backed away. Out of the corner of my eye, I saw Augustine, looking at the scene stricken. He was by an open door that the others seemed to have already gone through. He knew that Shyann was down, and I was alone to face the dragon. "I will stand on Ceriphina's behalf, Zaphn," the heir-not-to-be challenged the dragon.

"You? Augustine, you are far less of a threat to me than Shyann is. You could very certainly die," Zaphn answered him.

I gasped. I didn't want Augustine to die. I didn't want anyone to die today, especially Augustine.

Augustine waited a minute before he responded. "At least I will die honorably." He sighed.

"No!" I shouted. In that moment, I realized that I considered Augustine like family. He was my friend, someone I could trust with my secrets. And I didn't want him to die.

No! Zaphn, this has already gone too far! Won't you listen? Is this what I get for being too late? Please, stop what you are doing! Don't commit an action here and now that you will regret. I know you've already done so, though. But stop it. Don't do something you will regret.

Zaphn turned around to face the heir-not-to-be. Augustine tensed and drew his sword, preparation for what he knew would come.

But the dragon stood still. He stayed there for a moment.

Zaphn didn't attack physically. But what he said, Augustine could not have prepared for in the moment he was given.

"I tell you the truth, Augustine, and it is something that you have dreaded for a time," Zaphn said mysteriously. Augustine gripped the handle of his sword tighter, but his worry was clear by the way the tip of the blade trembled. Zaphn was right. This was something that Augustine didn't want to hear. And the only thing I could think of that Augustine would dread was …

"Zinnune holds you accountable for what you have done," the dragon whispered clearly.

That was it. That was the final blow for Augustine. His sword dropped to the floor and clattered, the only noise in the room. Words were more powerful than any hit Zaphn could strike. The dragon had played his cards well. He had won this battle.

Ugh … I heard from Shyann. She was rousing, but I wasn't sure if I wanted her to see the destruction Zaphn had wreaked upon us.

Then the dragon turned to me again. He stepped forward, and I backed away. My back was to the wall quickly, but Zaphn didn't stop. He kept coming closer.

"No ..." Shyann whispered painfully.

Zaphn stopped coming when he was a few feet away. "So you have woken, Shyann. Just in time to witness your defeat." He growled ominously.

I could feel Shyann stiffen. *Wh-what will ... you ... do ... Zaphn ... ?*

"Have ... mercy ... Zaphn," Shyann whispered. "Please ... do not ... hurt ... Ceriph."

"You are weak, Shyann. You have lost this battle." Zaphn was degrading her, eroding her like a river eventually turns a stone into sand.

Then the dragon snatched me up into the air with his claws. "No!" Shyann gasped. I screamed.

"Shyann, you cannot save your precious Ceriph," Zaphn said softly. Then he took off into the air to the broken air duct. "At least, you can only save one of them."

I looked down. Augustine was right below the air duct. If Zaphn collapsed the duct, it would fall upon Augustine.

He realized this too. "Shyann, save Ceriphina!" he shouted.

"What about you?" I asked. I was paralyzed by this. If Zaphn brought stone from the ceiling down, Augustine would be crushed. That would feel like losing Sane all over again.

Augustine didn't answer.

Suddenly, Zaphn thrust me to the ground and let go. I was falling fast. *No ...*

"Ceriphina!" Shyann called. She pushed off the wall and ran to me. She jumped into the air and turned so her back was facing the floor. Her wings outspread, even the broken one, she stopped my fall with her body.

Then we both hit the ground, Shyann as my buffer.

Shyann shouted at the impact. Her broken wing must had been jarred heavily.

"Lord, help me ... get everyone ... in this ... room ... to safety ..." she cried out.

Augustine went over to us. I crawled off of Shyann, but not before I felt her go limp again.

"She's unconscious," I said.

Then I heard the sound of metal screeching and stone cracking and breaking above us. Zaphn was out of sight, but he clearly had collapsed the air duct and the rock above us.

"Dear God, HELP US!" I shouted. There was nothing I could do. None of this was in my control. It was in the Lord Almighty's hand. Only He could save us now.

The rock and metal came closer and closer. I turned my back and covered my head, awaiting the rubble to puncture my skin.

Chapter 16

Onwards

It never came.

I looked around. There was no rubble. We weren't even in the room. We were in a hallway. I saw the back of a lab coat further down. Alexion. And Masseran and Ralloy too.

Ralloy was facing us and was looking at us in surprise. Did just we appear out of nowhere? I suppose it doesn't really matter. I'm just glad that I'm alive.

Masseran and Alexion turned to face us. Alexion came to us. "Are you okay?" he asked.

"I don't know, but Shyann is hurt. Badly, I think," I told him. "Are you a doctor too?"

Alexion took a good look at Shyann. Augustine and I stepped back as he gingerly turned her so that she was on her chest. "That *is* bad. I assume that Zaphn inflicted it?" Alexion observed. I nodded. "That makes sense. I believe they are fierce enemies."

That looked true. And Zaphn sure wasn't trying to help that improve.

"We need a splint for it. There is not much else I can do," he said.

Augustine began taking off his belt. "Here. You can use my scabbard and belt." The heir-not-to-be gave them to Alexion. He nodded his thanks, then began splinting Shyann's wing into the right position.

It was done in less than a minute. "If I had the materials, I would have cleaned it," Alexion stated. "She should keep pressure off her back, I think. I haven't done this before," he admitted.

"It's the best we got," Masseran said. "We need a plan to stop the storm of anger."

Alexion brightened. "I am in full agreement. But I could not intentionally make design flaws in the storm, except for the eye of the storm."

"How does a storm have design flaws?" Ralloy spoke up.

"I heard the conversation between Shyann and Zaphn. I believe that Ceriphina may be vital to the operation." Alexion motioned to me.

As a shield and arrow ... Now I get it. Zaphn saw me as Ralloy's protector, someone who could stop the storm of anger before it began.

I remembered my dream last night and the orange snowflakes I saw outside. I shuddered. It felt like the storm had already begun.

And Shyann didn't understand *as an arrow*. Maybe Zaphn meant that he knew that I could stop the storm if it happened. That was why he was threatening me. And that was why he was degrading Shyann. If he got through Shyann, he could get to me. It was scary to think about what he would do if that happened.

"This could end badly," Masseran stated. Somehow, she still had her cello and its bow intact. "Either we destroy the storm and avert the war or we end up with a dangerous storm and Liberators' War II."

"We might end up with Liberators' War II anyway," Alexion mentioned bluntly.

"That's not helpful," Shyann said.

I released a breath that I didn't realize that I had been holding. Shyann had risked so much for me, and I was grateful for it.

"Are you feeling okay?" I asked her.

"He beat me up worse seven years ago. Today, it was battle with words. Mostly." Shyann groaned. "I'm not sure what hurts more—his words or the pain. Words hurt too." She pointed to her heart. "They are arrows to here."

I got the analogy. Words can inflict more pain than a physical wound. I saw that with Augustine clearly.

"I'm just glad that you are unharmed," Shyann said.

I looked down to my chest. The words Zaphn spoke hurt me too. I thought that he would kill Augustine. "Not entirely unharmed," I told Shyann. I knew she understood even though she didn't say anything in response.

I stood up. Shyann did too. "Let us go onward now," she said.

"Where?" Masseran asked even though I thought that we all knew by now.

"Can I say something?" Augustine interrupted. Ralloy nodded.

"Varnillon is gathering an army, but Ruofen hasn't told you why. He told me, and I think I am at liberty to reveal it to you now," Augustine said to us.

"Shyann, Ruofen told me that you said that the Oppression was planning an attack. At first, I saw no reason for them to attack, other than conquest. But the storm provides them with the opportunity for war," Augustine told us. Shyann nodded.

"That explains *how* they'll start the war. How did they figure it out?" Masseran said.

"The Oppression had seven years to figure that out," Alexion answered her rather bluntly.

It was silent for a minute. That settles it. The storm is connected directly to Ralloy. And this has to do with the Oppression, not the Barnillon.

"I think we should move now," Augustine said. We began walking.

Suddenly, we were outside. *An invisible Pathway. Again.*

It was snowing, but this was no ordinary snow. The flakes were as big as my hand and a scarlet color. They were falling in slow motion.

"The storm has already begun," Alexion said. I figured that out already.

"What do we do?" Shyann asked, determined.

"We go for the eye of the storm," Alexion responded.

Chapter 17

Destroyed

DID HE MEAN LITERALLY OR Ralloy? There was no way that Alexion could know about Ralloy's connection with the storm. He simply didn't know Ralloy well enough to connect the dots. Except for Ralloy himself, I could be the only one that knew the truth about the eye of the storm.

Then Ralloy sprang forward and sprinted into the forest.

"Ralloy!" Augustine cried out. He began running after him. I ran after him, and the others followed.

I dodged trees and giant red snowflakes that were growing by the second. They streaked faster and faster. They grew more plentiful, and my sight was obscured. I felt a little panicky as I groped around for a tree or something to hang onto.

I found my tree soon enough. I held onto it tightly.

"SHYANN!" I shouted. "AUGUSTINE! SOMEBODY, CAN YOU HEAR ME?" I called into the wind that was picking up. Fear crept into my heart as the wind howled and screeched. What if no one heard me? The snow was cold even through my armor-parka. It wasn't what I expected, but that was how it was.

Dear God, please give me hope. Shyann, I could hear Shyann. *Please give me the courage to continue on with this battle. Zaphn's words really did hurt more than the pain he inflicted on me. Are they lies? If I believe them, then the battle of my mind will be lost. Help me to know the truth.*

Then I felt a feathery touch on my cheek. My fear was quickly relieved by hope because it was Shyann.

"Ceriphina? Are you there?" I heard her speak.

"Yes, I'm here!" I exclaimed.

"Good." I felt Shyann's hand on my shoulder. "I was afraid for you. Low visibility," she told me.

"Thanks," I replied. "Where are the others?"

"I cannot assure you that they are together now. But I wish to speak to you before we find them," Shyann answered.

"Okay," I responded. Shyann was silent for a moment.

"Do you think what Zaphn said about me … is true?" Shyann hesitantly questioned.

The question hit hard. It wasn't as painful as the Exposial dragon's direct words, but Shyann was admitting that she couldn't see the line between truth and lies that Zaphn had drawn. Shyann was wondering if she really was weak, like Zaphn said. After all, he had defeated her easily and fairly quickly in their most recent battle. Shyann was indeed doubting, but was strong enough to admit it.

There was a poem that seemed to fit Shyann's struggle. It didn't rhyme, but it was well-known throughout Setlia.

> "To whom will the victory go to?
> Light or darkness.
> The darkness forces;
> The light invites.
> It may appear at times that the dark is winning;

That evil is stronger than good;
But may I remind you
That it is the light that chases
The shadows from all its corners?
Yes, no matter how dark it may look, Shyann,
The light will always be
Victorious
In the end."

"You stood up to Zaphn, regardless of the consequences. You saved my life, even though it brought more physical pain. You told me, here and now, that you are struggling with this. Shyann, do you know what I say? I say, how can you be weak? Laying your life down for a friend takes immense courage and strength. I believe that you are strong, Shyann. You are strong and brave and courageous to me. And a friend," I finished.

Shyann took that in for a minute. "Thank you, Ceriph. I needed to hear that. I suppose that words can heal as well," she answered me. I felt a rising warmth inside of me. Shyann had said that words can hurt and words can heal. That was very true.

"Let's go to the others now," Shyann said. I stepped to where I thought she was and was pulled into one of her wings, the unbroken one. She moved toward a blue light, and I followed. The light rushed upon us, and I realized that we had gone through another Pathway. I still couldn't see well in the storm.

Then suddenly, the snow cleared for several yards. In my sight was a damaged AttackShift aircraft. A hole was ripped out of the entire back of the vehicle, which likely caused the crash to happen.

The crash site was new, but I saw no human there. At least, so far. "I don't see anyone."

"Do we *really* have to go through the whole is-it-an-elevator-or-closet thing again?" I heard from behind me. "Because, really, it gets annoying. If there's a—" But the AttackShift pilot couldn't finish because I was giving her a really tight hug.

"You can let me go now, Ceriph!" Enstar exclaimed. I did. "Whew! You have a really strong grip!" she told me.

I smiled even though I had never noticed before. Hugs were a rare thing for me ever since Sane went missing.

Enstar looked at Shyann, who had moved to my side. "I get the idea that it might be a miracle that you are still alive," she commented.

"How did you know?" was my query.

"It's not that hard to tell," Enstar replied, like it was obvious. I remembered Shyann's wing and winced. It really was.

"How did you get here?" I asked.

"First, I lost the vehicle I was in. Then I lost the parachute. Then I lost the backpack the parachute came in. At least I was close to the ground when the parachute ripped," Enstar commented. AttackShift aircraft came in different sizes, but always had magnetic wings or whatever that hovered close to the main control cockpit. This one had apparently lost both of them in the air, along with the back of the cockpit. "As for how I crashed, I think a dragon tore up the main magnetizing modulator in the back. That's the only thing big enough to damage an AttackShift aircraft in a future war zone. Not sure who, because there aren't many dragons of any species in Caredest," the pilot explained. "At least it wasn't a passenger plane."

It had to be Zaphn, but why would he attack an AttackShift aircraft? Sure, the pilot is Ralloy's cousin, and Ralloy is the eye of the storm, and getting to him would mean getting to me, but how would Zaphn *know* it was Enstar flying? I don't know if he even knew she was piloting, and if he didn't, it would be random. Unless he wanted to destroy all flying objects in the area. Aside from the snowflakes.

"I have a medical kit that has a better splint, Shyann. Would you like me to replace the one you have on your wing?" Enstar offered.

"You are a doctor who can treat this?" Shyann asked.

"I have a license and a specialized splint. I'm not sure why I brought it along, but I suppose it was a good thing I did. You want it?" the pilot assured her. Shyann nodded. "Okay. I'll go get the kit." She went to the AttackShift aircraft and ducked through the hole in the back. She came out a few seconds later, holding a bag that looked like it was designed to be resistant to pretty much anything that would harm the medical supplies inside of it. Enstar sat down, so we did the same. She pulled out a short metal rod, a cleaning cloth, and a roll of bandages. Shyann moved over to Enstar and let her take off the makeshift splint. Enstar held her patient's wing in a natural flight position so it wouldn't hurt as much. If there was any pain, Shyann didn't show it. As Enstar put the rod—the specialized splint, apparently—in place, I wondered how many times Shyann had suffered at Zaphn's hand. How many wounds had he inflicted upon her? Did she bear any emotional scars from battles past? How long have Shyann and Zaphn been enemies? Ever since during the First Liberators' War? I don't know, and it didn't seem like the right time to ask her.

"There! We are done." Enstar finished wrapping the bandage around Shyann's wing, letting it dangle awkwardly as Shyann instinctively folded the other wing on her back.

"It feels awkward, but better." She acknowledged Enstar with a nod of gratitude. She stood up, and Enstar and I did too. It looked awkward too, but Shyann didn't seem to mind how she looked, and I didn't really mind either. She was a brave warrior and my friend.

"Should we go and find the others?" I asked Shyann.

"How many of you are there? Is anyone else hurt?" the doctor and pilot asked. Shyann shook her head, clearly not really wanting to explain the concept of the storm of anger that she might or m not actually understand. I wasn't sure if she had figured out the storm-Ralloy connection or not.

"Ooh! I just remembered!" Enstar exclaimed, then retrieved a familiar baton from the back of her belt. It was the gentle torch that she had with her when she found me, the torch that had broken the energetic barrier Shyann had been trapped inside. "I thought that you might need this even though I had no idea we were going to meet up. It's funny, right?" She handed the baton-torch to me. It was funny if you look at it like that, but I felt like that this was the Lord Almighty providing for us, helping us to actually destroy the storm of anger and prevent Liberators' War II.

Or just the storm of anger.

I fingered it, then held it tightly. "Thank you," I responded simply. Enstar grinned. It looked similar to Ralloy's grin from over seven years ago. Sorrow washed over me, because that was before all this. The Terrible Raid, the anger, the bitterness, the storm.

This was deeper than the potential war. I knew that Ralloy was the center of it … but what I didn't realize before is

105

that he would have to let it all go. If the storm was connected to Ralloy's anger, then he would have to stop being angry to stop the storm of anger.

That was something I'm not sure if he would do.

We walked through another one of Shyann's Pathways to get to a large tree that Augustine was at. Then we quickly found everyone else, except Ralloy.

At first, I mistook Enstar for Ralloy. His energy signal is strangely as widespread as the storm, so I cannot tell where he is now.

"Where's Ralloy?" Enstar queried. "He's here, right? Ceriphina wouldn't be here if he wasn't with you."

"I don't know where he is, but I have a theory," Augustine said. If he made any motions, the red snow obscured them. The wind wasn't as loud as before. "Alexion, where were the coordinates for the center of the storm? I have reason to believe that he is heading there."

"I believe that they were set on the Alsekan side of the Border Mount. We are still in Caredest, correct?"

"I would know if we were in Alseka. The storm will move in from there, onto Caredest?" Shyann said. She made it sound like the answer was yes.

"Do we have specific coordinates or an indicator if we're getting closer?" Augustine questioned.

"The snowflakes get larger and sharper the further in you go, or it comes to you. It is relatively similar to the structure of a hurricane," Alexion explained. "Why would he want to go to the eye of the storm? It is the most dangerous part of the storm ... and Zaphn may be there, for reasons I don't know."

This could *really* end bad then. If things get out of hand, I don't think Augustine acting as a wall will prevent

Ralloy from finally releasing all of his pent-up anger … in a dangerous way.

Or was the storm the indicator that he had already begun?

Zaphn is easier to notice than Ralloy at the moment. Shyann said to me specifically. *And I would be easier to notice for him.*

If Ralloy and Zaphn meet, then we come in bringing Shyann, then if Ralloy explodes …

The scene was set to be dangerous. The atmosphere is unstable and precarious. Tension is indeed thick within the air.

"Zaphn is indeed on the Alsekan side of the mountain. Alexion, if someone with the exact energy trace as the storm was traveling through it, how would the movement of the energy in the storm be?" Shyann asked. Science question.

"Indirect location? Good strategy. The movement would be something like an ocean current, if Ralloy is moving. He would be invisible on any standard energy radar if he was stagnant," Alexion explained. I doubt that Ralloy would stay still, though. Too unlikely at this point.

"The 'current' indicates that Ralloy is also on the other side of the border. His trajectory will soon meet Zaphn's trajectory," Shyann reported.

"Let's get going then," Augustine said.

Wait, Ceriphina. I think it would be best if you turn the torch on as we go through the Pathway. Shyann told me. I looked at the torch in its baton form. There weren't any buttons on it, and nothing else to turn it on. How did Enstar turn it on when she broke the energy barrier and freed Shyann? I didn't see her do it clearly.

"Enstar? How did you turn the torch on?" I blurted out.

"There's a sensor right below the part where it moves. You hold your thumb there for a second, then it opens to its full height," she explained to me.

Then Shyann opened the Pathway, and we walked through.

The first thing I noticed is that the snowflakes were bigger and sharper. They were moving faster with the fierce winds, dangerous projectiles streaming through the air. I turned on the gentle torch like Enstar said. It opened and expanded to the torch that she had when she found me. And surprisingly, the snowflakes began avoiding the torch's fire that blazed softly. It repelled them.

Hmm. Energetic science. And it kind of makes sense even though that was probably not in my grade level of energetic science. The storm of anger was made of energetic anger. I have no idea what energy the gentle fire had, but it was gentle and soothing and relaxing. The opposite of anger. So, of course, the gentle torch repelled the snowflakes.

And up ahead a few feet, in the midst of the storm, stood Ralloy. He was standing there, sword gripped tightly in his hand. His back was to us, but the arcs were on the hilt. The hot and stifling atmosphere was back. I heard nothing from him, though, as if he didn't notice us.

Augustine walked toward the young warrior and placed a hand on his shoulder. He gripped strong. "Stand down, Ralloy. Do not attack whoever else comes," he commanded, expressing his authority to him.

Zaphn has changed course. He is intentionally heading here, to Ralloy, most likely. He thinks that I have been defeated, but I have not. I will defend you and Ralloy from him, Shyann reported. She could protect us from Zaphn. But could she protect us from … Ralloy?

Then a familiar roar pierced the wind. Zaphn. The snowflakes averted from him as the Exposial dragon landed heavily on the ground. He stayed on all fours for a moment, apparently resting for some reason.

That moment was all it took for Ralloy to break Augustine's hold on his shoulder and start running toward the dragon, brandishing his arc-covered sword like he seriously was going to attack Zaphn.

"No!" Augustine exclaimed in surprise. Zaphn himself only appeared to notice the presence of his attacker when he was a few feet away. Ralloy swung at the dragon's neck. Zaphn blocked the blade extension with his right claw. He held it there for a second, then groaned softly and pushed it away slowly.

That must have been what Shyann meant by hesitancy when she told us of her battle with Zaphn when we first met. Like he didn't want to fight.

"You would dare do battle with me, Ralloy? You would fight a dragon with no shield? This is a different type of recklessness," Zaphn questioned Ralloy's decision. Like we all were doing.

Ralloy said nothing. He took fast breaths, and I could hear them.

The Exposial stood up on two legs, towering above Ralloy like a giant. "Well, then. Your choice has been made. You cannot stand down." Zaphn growled softly.

No one said anything. We were all on edge, relatively shocked by this.

The scene was set. The scene was now.

Chapter 18

A Different Type of Recklessness

"Is HE *THINKING STRAIGHT?*" ALEXION whispered as the dragon and young reckless warrior clashed. "Zaphn is correct. No person with even a shred of sanity would dare attack an Exposial dragon with no shield. *Especially* him."

"I don't think that he was thinking at *all*," Masseran drily commented.

The battle had moved on quickly. Ralloy and Zaphn had turned around ninety degrees … until Zaphn sprung into the air and flew up high. Ralloy lifted his head and yelled into the powerful downbeats. "COME DOWN HERE AND FIGHT ME LIKE A MAN, ZAPHN!" The young warrior's voice seemed to be lost to the wind.

"Now he's ignorant," the scientist said.

"Of the fact that Zaphn is a completely different species?" Masseran mentioned. "He doesn't fight like a man because he's a dragon. Not human. There's a very clear difference."

"Of Zaphn's battle technique with a grounded opponent. First, he ascends to such a height that the opponent believes that he has retreated, or decided that it wasn't worth it. Thus, the opponent drops his guard and starts to leave or begins yelling at the sky for him to fight nobly, like Ralloy is. Then after a while, Zaphn does come down … only to crush his enemy against the earth. He tried it on me, but it obviously failed," Alexion explained.

Yeah, we all were ignorant about that.

"So that means that it's about time for Ralloy to stop yelling and start making unpredictable movements." The heir-not-to-be grasped my wrist and gently pulled me back.

"Do not fear," he whispered.

Then Zaphn did come down to the ground.

Ralloy saw him, because he had kept his eyes on the sky the entire time. He wasn't yelling anymore but kept staring … and jumped out of the way seconds before the Exposial dragon collided with the ground.

The earth cracked at the impact. Snow came up like dust. It took some time for Zaphn to stir and get back on his feet. During Zaphn's possible unconscious moment, Ralloy didn't move toward Zaphn to declare victory. He didn't step back to us for "safety in numbers" or anything.

He stood still, right there. Unmoving. The arcs had disappeared from his sword.

When all was still, I could hear Ralloy's fast, shallow breaths.

Ralloy had come to his senses.

Ralloy was not angry anymore.

He was scared.

That's not necessarily a *good* thing, though.

And to add to the number of events, it's getting uncomfortably hot over here. Not so much of a good thing either.

Zaphn finally rose from the reddish-orange snow. And to say he looked mad was an understatement. He shook off the snow and outstretched his wings. Then he roared and gave a fierce look at all of us.

Zaphn now bore a wound on his tail. Slices and shallow cuts decorated his forearms and shins. There was also a large gash at the base of his neck, but the dragon seemed to take that as nothing. What really looked as if it bothered him was the crash into the ground, as he wasn't focusing on any one of us. Bruises were beginning to form on the impact area on Zaphn's main body.

Ralloy, on the other hand, was bearing fewer wounds that I could see. His back was still toward us. The scratch from eight days ago seemed to be have been opened again, because he was looking down at his chest. Deeper claw marks marred his bulletproof armor and his arms around to the point where I could see them. That's all I could see. However, Ralloy *still* did not drop his sword in *any* type of surrender.

Neither of them made a move. It grew so silent that I could hear everyone's breathing again.

Until Zaphn roared. Everyone jumped as he rose to his back legs.

And then shot a stream of fire at Ralloy.

I closed my eyes tightly. I did not want to see this.

Seconds later, I heard Alexion. "Ceriphina, look!"

So I did.

My neighbor had been blown back a few feet. He was in a sitting position, like he had just fallen. He was still holding his sword.

And he had not burned.

Zaphn summed up my reaction—almost everyone's reactions—in one sentence.

"I had forgotten that you are a Lyre," Zaphn rumbled icily. He was breathing heavily.

Then the dragon walked over to an obviously shaking Ralloy. Zaphn then quickly snatched the fourteen-year-old warrior up by his parka that was covering his armor. He steadied his feet, turning to an angle at which we could clearly see what he was going to do. Zaphn grasped Ralloy's hood with his other claw and tore it along with the parka off Ralloy. He instinctively slashed at Zaphn's wrist, cutting a deep wound, but dropped his sword in the process. Zaphn, however, acted as if he felt nothing. He changed the claw he was holding his captive in and raised his now-free claw above his head.

Zaphn growled lowly. His raised claw then appeared to turn white, like a visible blade extension. It looked—and felt—dangerous. Possibly even lethal. An attack that I knew I couldn't—would not allow Zaphn to do.

"No!" I shouted, reaching with my hand. "Please, don't do this!"

Zaphn, no. A stern voice—the same one from the laboratory—said. *Listen to her and do not do this.*

Zaphn stared at Ralloy. Nothing was said between them. Shyann said nothing to me.

And Zaphn dropped the attack, the extension disappearing into thin air. Zaphn listened to me.

But to be honest, the adverse wasn't much better.

Acting as if his index claw was sword point, Zaphn brought his arm down ... and held it at my friend Ralloy's throat.

Chapter 19

A Severe Threat

ZAPHN WAS STARING INTENSELY AT Ralloy. "I never thought it would have come to this. I really thought that Lindsair's family was smarter than this … to not ever get in this situation, what humans would say is a mess. I did not think you were reckless. But it seems I have underestimated you, and you have underestimated me. But no more!" the Exposial dragon confessed. Ralloy said nothing.

But he didn't continue; instead, he hesitated for an unknown reason.

I took that moment. I ran determined toward the dragon. This was probably the most reckless thing I ever did in my life. But there was a life in the balance.

So I kept running. Shyann didn't say a word. She was watching me. She understood me and didn't question me. No one else cried out because Shyann didn't.

Shyann thought I could make it.

And that fueled my courage. So I kept running, faster and faster as I got closer.

Then when I was close enough, I leaped—impossibly so—upon Zaphn's side and grabbed hold of a spine with my free hand.

I grabbed one of Zaphn's spines as the dragon roared at the impact. I must have hit the bruised area. Zaphn whirled his head and long neck around to look at me. "You too, Ceriphina? You too would risk your life to take on a certainly *fatal* challenge for a companion?" he questioned.

It's not like I'm just going to sit around and watch Zaphn kill Ralloy! Of course I would do this! Regardless!

"Of course I would," I answered. "Why would I do anything else?"

He kept glaring at me, and I kept up my determination. And for a second, he actually looked *amazed*, like he couldn't believe my choice. Then he roared again and jumped into the air and gave a powerful downbeat. He slowly jerked higher, and each wingbeat threatened to make me lose my grip on the spine. On a particularly forceful one, possibly a few thousand feet in the air, my hand slipped, and a short descent ended when I gripped Zaphn again, this time mid-leg. The Exposial was definitely trying to shake me off. "Let us test this falling theory!" Zaphn roared wildly. Maybe I knew what he meant.

I could occasionally spot Shyann, flying stiffly, painfully, and impossibly, trying to fit in an attack while not hurting me or Ralloy, but Zaphn was jerking around too much for her to do so. It appeared that she kept searching though.

Zaphn made a sudden drop again, and I dropped down and grabbed his ankle. But the jolt made me lose my grip on the torch, and I watched it fall to the faraway ground below. Well, there goes physical defense. Not a good thing. I was getting nervous. Was this a bad idea? It really was looking like it, but there was nothing I could do about my decision.

And was it me, or did the sky look *plain different*?

Then Zaphn kicked me into the air and caught my snow armor in the abdomen with his free claw (well, it wasn't free anymore). He then held me alongside Ralloy.

My neighbor had not spoken or even moved a muscle since Zaphn took off. Even afraid, this was unlike him. He would have shouted for everyone to stay back or at least called for help at this point. Or maybe yell in fear.

A good look at the warrior told me the truth. It looked like he was stirring from fainting, and his skin appeared to be red and dry. He was sweaty, which should have been expected, but he looked like he was drenched. His chest indicated fast, shallow breaths.

It looked like he had heat stroke.[1]

Ralloy's squinting eyes seemed unfocused for a minute. Then he opened them wide and turned his head to face me. It took longer than it should have to realize I was there. "I … felt … like … I should … look … here … but … is anyone … there?" he said to no one. He probably didn't realize Zaphn was there either.

"Silence." Zaphn growled softly.

Ralloy paid no attention, as he said, "Ceri … phina? … You … are … that … is … you … right? I … feel … dizzy … and … my … heart … is … pum … ping … too … fast … and … and I … feel … hotter than … normal …" He struggled to speak. Tears were forming in his eyes as he outstretched his arm to me. This had never happened before. Ralloy had never spoken to me much before, much less admit weakness. The short conversation we had right before Enstar freed Shyann was the most we had in years. Whether he was aware that he

---

[1] Since I am not a doctor, I had to do a little research on heat stroke. I got the information on heat stroke from www.webmd.com.

was in the claws of the most powerful Exposial dragon or not, he never would have told anyone of pain. But now, he was. There was a real problem, and Ralloy truly felt genuine.

Zaphn separated us further. But he glanced fearfully at the warrior. Zaphn could feel Ralloy's body heat. Could Ralloy have absorbed the heat from Zaphn's fire somehow? If that were true, Ralloy could possibly be *burning from the inside out.*

Zaphn's eyes said he was thinking the same thing. It clearly troubled him.

Then Shyann flew and hovered right in front of Zaphn's nose. "Hand Ralloy and Ceriphina to me, Zaphn. They are not yours," she commanded, but her facade was see-through. She knew Zaphn wouldn't obey. She knew he could drop us and battle her and win while we were taken care of for good. She was taking a great risk, and now we need it.

"Shyann? I thought you would never gather the strength to show your face to me again. Yet here you are … today is a day of surprises. You are already weakened for air combat, but nevertheless, you also will risk everything for people? They can do *nothing* for you," Zaphn prompted.

Shyann didn't seem offended by the insult. "That is where your thinking is wrong, Zaphn," she said bluntly and boldly. A glance at Zaphn told he was shocked that *anyone* would confront him like this … that Shyann would confront him. He was used to enemies cowering in fear, knowing that they would be utterly defeated, and using that fear against them. That might have been Shyann before, but that was not the Shyann today. She might be physically and emotionally hindered, but she was spiritually courageous—energetic doesn't count, so that's the only option left. Shyann knows God and knows Him well enough to trust that He will protect her from further harm. "Humanity has done plenty to me. Help and hurt, it doesn't matter, for it only contributes to my strength today. And that is why I will assist these two now. So listen to me, Zaphn," Shyann said boldly. All hints of fear were gone. She stared the dragon in the eye. "Your species was designed to know truth and make it known to *all* species. Yet here you are, abusing your power. You are threatening to kill teenagers! What has happened to the integrity of you and the Exposial dragons? What happened to your honor?"

Zaphn lunged threateningly at Shyann. "Listen to *me*, Prisoner X! I do not need or want a second Pachelbel! Stop trying to win me back to the Liberators!" He then threw Ralloy into the air and pointed. "If verbal battle is what I wanted, I would have gone to him myself!" he roared. Shyann had already caught Ralloy at this point, but her altitude had dropped and was struggling to ascend back to her former height.

"Face it, Prisoner X. You cannot come back up in your condition … with your burden, that is. It would be faster to *let go*," Zaphn crudely offered.

"No, Zaphn. I will get there, and I *will* … be … *healed in the power of the Lord Almighty!*"

It was then her wing beats evened out, and Shyann's downbeats began to get altitude. It didn't look effortless, but her wing looked completely healed.

Wow. That is faith. *Huge* faith.

"Whaaat?" Zaphn sounded dumbfounded. He must have never seen this type of thing before firsthand. Or on any hand. Zaphn seriously underestimated the power of God Almighty. Seriously.

"Ceri … phina? … I … am … so … sorry … Can … you … forgive … me?" Ralloy was trying hard to compete with the wind of Zaphn's wings.

"You took Ralloy's anger as betrayal, Prisoner X!" the Exposial dragon shouted much louder than necessary. He sounded desperate. "What you take as betrayal you take as an attack to the heart! You should be weak! YOU ARE WEAK, SHYANN! DO YOU HEAR ME! YOU ARE WEAK, *SO YOU HAVE LOST!*" Zaphn roared so loud I'm surprised I'm not deaf.

"Ceri ... phina ... forgive ... me!" Ralloy yelled and gasped. He grimaced and put a hand to his forehead.

Shyann stared strong. "*Really?* Is that true? You know, I was taught something today. I learned that it doesn't matter what people say. It doesn't matter what other species say. It does not matter what *you* say. What the Lord Almighty says overrides all that. You told me my own species would despise me for my recklessness, but the Lord says they won't. You gave me a message—a *lie*—of hopelessness when I saw you again, that there was nothing I could do to stop you. I will confess, I truly did believe the lie. I felt like you had won the battle before it began. That this story could not be turned around."

"For ... give ... me ... for ... I ..."

"But He showed me that there is a hope, there *is* a light. No matter what."

"For ... the ... center ... the ... eye ... of ... the ... storm ... of ... anger ..."

"And now you say I am weak and defeated. *Again.* Do you think I would believe the same lie twice? Told in the same day? Don't you think that is *impossible?*"

"I pushed ... away what ... I needed ... most. The ... Lord Almighty ... and ... you. I ... won't do ... it any ... more ... but you ... need ... to know ... that ..."

"That is what I have learned. So do not try to *win me back*, Zaphn. And I am *not* Prisoner X!" Shyann concluded confidently.

"The eye of … the storm is … not … Zaphn … It is … I. I am … sorry. Will you … accept my … apology … and … forgive me? … For bring … bringing … all this … upon you … Ceriphina? … Can you?" Ralloy hung his head. Tears fell to the far ground below. Ralloy …

He wanted this as much as Augustine wanted it from his brother Zinnune. They were both desperate for forgiveness, like Zaphn was desperate to defeat us and Shyann. He would feel devastated, like Augustine would, if forgiveness was refused.

I opened my mouth to reply, but Zaphn made his next move right then and there.

And that move was *casting me down to the Setlian earth!*

"AHHHHHHH!" I yelled and panicked. Could I survive such a fall? Could I?

I. Don't. Know.

Zaphn roared again. "You have survived an extraordinary fall today, Ceriphina. So LET US TEST *THE LIMITS!*"

Fear heightened as I descended and turned headfirst. Shyann suddenly caught me, and Ralloy *kept* falling. Shyann strained to catch him too, but he was too far below us for it. Finally, Shyann gave up when the ground was too close to catch Ralloy. She wrapped her feathered wings in a conelike shape, put her arms around me tightly, and turned so that she would bear the impact.

I opened my eyes and saw a white sky. Where was I again? And why is there music?

"You're awake." A Zerhali man wearing armor came to my side. He seemed relieved that I was awake.

"What happened?" I asked.

"You, Shyann, and Ralloy fell from the sky after Zaphn roared, and he hit Shyann on her shoulder blades. That made her drop Ralloy and risked a serious head and brain injury protecting you from certain death. Unfortunately, she couldn't rescue Ralloy without losing you. So he is in an uncertain condition," a young woman with hair like fire, wearing a red uniform, explained. "It's a miracle in itself that all of you are alive."

Wait a minute … That sounded familiar. I had survived an extensive fall recently. Was that today? Was it eight days ago?

My head pounded. I groaned.

"For … given? Of … course …"

I didn't remember anything about forgiven, yet I was forgiven. But who did I need to give my forgiveness to? Was it Shyann? Or Ralloy? I felt like my head was swimming in a storm.

You interfered, Pachelbel. Even though you promised you would not, a vaguely familiar voice said. It sounded like a … dragon?

I did not interfere. I have never made contact with nor Probed Shyann. So you cannot accuse me of lying. It was a second dragon, but I didn't know who he was. His voice was gentler and smoother than the first, whose was harsher and rougher.

She sounded too much like you. That is why I am accusing you, Pachelbel! Was the second dragon Pachelbel?

How do you think I would have gotten here before you? This is unfamiliar territory.

For Voice.

Voices talking about a guy named Voice. It's ironic.

"What was that?" I asked numbly.

"What was what?" the Zerhali man asked.

"The voices. They sounded like dragons," I explained vaguely.

121

"It seems that physics are being defied at every turn," a Russian voice stated as if he was worried.

Voices? Of dragons?

Wake up, Ceriphina! A surge of unnecessary heat flooded my chest. Really? Another voice with *heat*? That's what's annoying.

Did they mention a name? Possibly Pachelbel?

It flooded back to me. Everything. Ralloy was the warrior who had attacked Zaphn, a powerful Exposial dragon who was a fear manipulator, and nearly died in the process. I had tackled the dragon when he threatened to take Ralloy's life, and Shyann had proved Zaphn's lies wrong. And we had all nearly died when he dropped me.

I groggily climbed to my feet. None of my companions bothered to stop me. I scanned the area for the torch of gentle flame that I had dropped. I saw where Shyann and I must have hit the reddish-orange snow. I saw the torch, and it was right next to Ralloy in its baton form.

I walked over to him and picked up the torch. I didn't activate it yet. I just went on one knee and examined him. He was unconscious, yet his eyes were open.

Ralloy was indeed overheating. He was still red. Claw marks circled his forearms. His chest wound had opened.

"Is he …" I began but couldn't bring myself to finish.

"He's breathing, but it is fast and shallow. He appears to have heat stroke," Alexion answered. Enstar nodded as confirmation. "At the same time, Ralloy is in shock or something like it. Nevertheless, he needs immediate treatment."

"I'll get snow!" Enstar started to leave.

"Due to the storm of anger, there is likely no proper snow on this side of the mountain," Alexion stated. "Sorry," he added as an afterthought.

"Oh. Okay," Enstar said and walked back. Then she did something—something very surprising for calm and collected Enstar. "THEN WHAT ON SETLIA ARE WE GOING TO DO? I CAN'T DO A THING! I CAN'T LET RALLOY DIE!" the AttackShift pilot screamed at the sky. "HE'S MY COUSIN!" Then she collapsed onto her knees and began crying.

"I'm afraid to say that I cannot do anything either," Alexion said softly. He was nervous to say it by the shaking in his voice.

"And I am not a physician," Augustine said and came closer.

True. Enstar was a doctor. But unless Shyann did it, there would be no way to get snow from the opposite side of Mount Thias. Or get Ralloy to someone who could help, not without putting him in risk. And if one of us went to Varnillon, Ralloy might not survive the whole time.

The cello music stopped abruptly. I stood and turned around. Masseran had dropped her cello in the red snow. "Well, how did Shyann's wing get healed?" she proposed.

"Shock and heat stroke do not relate with a broken wing, Masseran," Alexion said.

"They both hurt."

"She had faith," I said simply.

"Okay," Masseran replied just as simply. I began to worry if she even knew what I meant.

Then she cupped her hands around her mouth, turned around 180 degrees, and shouted at the sky too.

It took a second to recognize what she was saying as English or even words. But when I could, this is what I heard: "SEND A PHYSICIAN, GOD! PLEASE GIVE US SOMEONE WHO CAN DO SOMETHING!"

Chapter 20

Healing

WHY DIDN'T SHE ASK FOR the direct healing?

Suddenly, a shadow passed quickly overhead. We all looked up to the sky but I couldn't see the original flying object. Instead, There was ...

Zaphn!?

The Exposial dragon landed softly several yards away. Now that he was closer, I could see that Zaphn's identifying burn scar was absent on this dragon, as well as his dagger spine on his forehead. He also looked straight ahead, not even trying to look at us. The leather of this dragon's wings was white, not the soft gray of Zaphn's.

Everyone was silent. Even Enstar stopped yelling. No one knew how to take this new dragon. Alexion was probably happy it wasn't Zaphn.

But who was he?

"Is this the site of the storm of anger?" he asked. He sounded a lot like the second voice I heard earlier.

If the second dragon's voice belonged to Pachelbel, was *this* Pachelbel?

Big *if*.

I nodded to answer his question. Nobody spoke. The dragon didn't either. He waited a while before I realized that he was blind. *That* was why he was staring straight ahead.

He was also more patient than the other of his species that I had met.

"Yes. This is the site," I answered verbally. The dragon turned his head to me. Instinctively, I stepped back, but he didn't notice. He spoke again.

"I thought so. The wind patterns indicated a severe storm system, but I needed a second human's input."

Hmm. He certainly was comfortable with people—at least one. I think.

"Is there a person suffering of a heat injury? I may have a way to help," the dragon offered. It sounded truthful. But was it?

"YES! YES! WHAT DO YOU NEED TO DO?" Enstar cried in joy. Beethoven's "Ode to Joy" began playing on Masseran's cello. I glanced at Augustine and Alexion. Alexion was smiling. Augustine looked more comfortable than before.

"Well … it involves the gentle torch," he replied. He carefully motioned to me and the gentle torch.

Wait a minute. "How did you know that I'm holding it?" I asked.

"An energetic telasclisior" was the answer. Probably like indirect location.

"May I use the gentle torch, please?" the Exposial dragon asked. He didn't reach his claws for it, but I tightened my grip on it anyway. I just wanted to know one thing beforehand.

"What is your name?" I said as I stepped forward.

"My name is Pachelbel," he answered promptly. Now Pachelbel outstretched his right arm and stepped forward.

He must have misjudged where I was, though, because he stopped a few feet away. I covered the remaining distance. I loosened my hold on the torch and held it out in my right hand. My hand settled on Pachelbel's, and I tried to give him a handshake. It wasn't working, but Pachelbel got the idea and gave a gentle one.

"I'm Ceriphina," I introduced myself and smiled. As I withdrew my hand, I left the torch in Pachelbel's claws.

Pachelbel gave sort of an awkward smile. "It is a happy surprise that you trust me, Ceriphina. I would not have blamed you if you did not," the Exposial dragon said softly.

Then he activated it much faster than I thought he would have been able to. But who am I to complain? Pachelbel balanced it horizontally at his eye level, and the gentle fire slowly retreated into the torch.

Then Pachelbel pointed the empty torch at Ralloy.

I jumped back, unsure of *what the torch was supposed to be doing.*

Enstar and Alexion dropped down to Ralloy, checking his temperature by hand. Pachelbel gave a soft groan as he dropped the torch and swayed a little. He had to step back to regain his balance.

Suddenly, a giant red snowflake zoomed toward Pachelbel. He definitely noticed it and batted at it as if it were a fly. It wasn't what people do, though, because when the Exposial dragon hit it, it *shattered to its individual atoms.* That's what it looked like. It would be a fatal blow if a living creature got in the way.

"He's freezing now, but that's because of the shock," Enstar announced worriedly. It was getting colder now.

"Three hundred degrees? It should have been impossible even for a Lyre to survive at such temperatures!" Pachelbel exclaimed wearily.

Surviving three hundred degrees of internal body heat is basically a flat-out *miracle.*

"He's in shock too? I am sorry, but you need a doctor for that recovery. I unfortunately cannot help at this point." Pachelbel sighed. "Hope to see you again."

Then without further ado, the dragon took off.

"Huh. How are we going to find a doctor that's not treating someone from either of the armies?" Augustine asked.

"Well ... I know a physician ..." Alexion began saying. He seemed nervous. Very nervous.

"Where?" we all asked. Hopefully, the doctor was close by and not on the other side of Setlia.

"On the opposite side of Varnillon," the scientist continued.

"Is there anything else we need to know?" Augustine asked. He spotted a snowflake heading toward him and blocked it with his sword. It might have been easier if he had ducked, though, because the snowflake drove into the one-inch-thick blade. Augustine forced the blade in, and the snowflake's halves fluttered to the snow-covered ground. "These snowflakes are dangerous," he commented, showing us the damage the snowflake did. It had cleanly cut the tip off the blade.

"This is the point where you stop asking me questions," Alexion said wearily. "As for the doctor ... Two things. The first is that he is an Oppressionist," Alexion went on.

"How do you *know* an Oppressionist in Varnillon in the first place?" Enstar inquired from her position of spearing another snowflake in midair with Ralloy's sword. The snowflake disintegrated.

Alexion ducked as yet another snowflake whirled toward us. We all followed. "As for the second thing, it also answers Enstar's inquiry," Alexion said.

"The physician ... is my father."

Chapter 21

Pleading with Father

My jaw opened a little when I heard that.

Then I remembered that Alexion was locked in the laboratory. Alone. To design the thing that he wanted to destroy. He had been forced. But he never said who …

Because it must have been his father.

But what could have destroyed the bond between father and son?

"Duck!" Alexion yelled suddenly. Then he did just that. We did too. I heard the snowflake pass overhead from the opposite direction the previous one was going. Could it be the same one?

Shyann came out of the sky suddenly and destroyed the snowflake with her bare hands. She came over to me. I went down on my knees beside Ralloy. I fitted my hand, then my arm, between Ralloy's arm and back and other arm. I lifted his upper body so he was in a sitting position. He kept staring ahead and groaned a bit. "Ceriph … ? You … will … right?" he said, barely above a whisper.

"Rest, okay? We're going to go to a doctor who can help." *I just hope he's willing to.* I slid my other arm under Ralloy's

129

knees and lifted. He was heavy, but Shyann must have been able to tell, because she came to my right side and helped me with his legs. Together, we lifted him so I was standing on my feet. Augustine helped me with the other side.

Ralloy was *very* cold. As if he had been inside a true blizzard and survived.

Shyann definitely noticed. "We need to get Ralloy to the physician immediately. He cannot remain in this condition for much longer," she said.

Enstar picked up the torch. "Well, what are we waiting for? Let's get going fast!" she shouted as she did just that. We all tried, but even Masseran (who somehow was *still* carrying her cello and its bow) was having an easier time keeping up pace with the AttackShift pilot. Alexion was staying with our pace and was saying something quietly in what I guessed was Russian. He didn't explain what it was, and Augustine probably didn't understand Russian or didn't want to translate, because no one did. So we kept on going, with Enstar battling all the snowflakes in our way, as we continued slowly but surely toward Varnillon and Alexion's father.

A full hour has passed since we began. It felt like years of trudging through snow. Many prayers have been said, asking for a miracle, that Ralloy could hang on to life as we traveled on.

We were walking through our neighborhood, a few streets away from my empty home. We were taking a main road, but I didn't see any soldiers or infantry or anything. Helicopters of battle clashed against various AttackShift vehicles, with occasional aircraft on either side dropping permanently out of the fight. The Zynkosiacs darted in every now and then, doing something that helped. Occasionally, I could hear and feel an energetic blast from the Oppression.

From what device, I don't know, but nobody explained. We kept on moving on, through snow that was now the color of dust. Left, right, left, right, left, right, left, right …

Then explosion several blocks away.

We were thrust forward by the force of it. Augustine, Shyann, and I were on our knees to prevent Ralloy from even falling an inch above the dust-colored snow. At this, Ralloy stirred from unconsciousness and said, "Home?" in a small voice. I didn't answer but looked back at the source of the explosion as we stood to our feet. I couldn't see where it had occurred, but I got a sick feeling deep down. Ralloy hadn't been *asking*.

He knew the explosive had hit both of our homes.

Then I heard a shout. It sounded like Alexion's whispering, so it might have been Russian. Now, if Alexion's father lived on the other side of the city and I lived (or technically used to) in the central area, then why would Alexion's father (or I think it is) be here of all places?

Never mind. At least it places the doctor closer to us!

"Thank God!" I said. Then I looked at Alexion.

It looked like he recognized the voice. But he didn't seem even a microscopic bit *happy* about it. He appeared to be very, *very* nervous.

"What's wrong, Alexion?" Augustine asked, concerned.

"Well … to be honest, before, I did not choose the Oppression … myself. My father … forced me to join it, although I preferred the Liberators. And he also arranged for me to assist Zaphn in designing the storm—duck!" he interrupted. We did, and a snowflake flew overhead. It looked larger than the others. "Well, my working with Zaphn was forced," the scientist continued. "I did not like it, and Zaphn did not enjoy working with someone who was anti-Oppression either. We frequently argued, and that resulted in Zaphn attacking me," Alexion said mournfully. "My relationship with my father crumbled to the atomic level, exactly what Zaphn was going to do to Ralloy. My father locked me inside that room where you found me," he continued. "I am not anticipating meeting my father again, especially because it is a Lyre that needs attention," he finished.

"Oh," Enstar said and looked down. "You were strong with Zaphn. Why not now?" she asked gingerly.

Alexion hung his head. "You do not understand. I was *pretending* with Zaphn. I knew he could see through me, but he played along. My father ... is different. He is a physician by trade, but he thinks like a scientist. He will not be convinced easily and likely refuse to see me." He sighed. We heard another shout in Russian.

"Well ... why is he calling now?" I asked.

"Good question. Very good question," Alexion said as he walked behind me and placed a gentle trembling hand on my shoulder. "I don't know."

The voice called out again. Alexion finally shouted a reply in Russian. It was silent for a long while. Not even one snowflake came near us in that period of time. The wind blew softly as an older man stepped from a nearby alleyway. As he slowly stepped forward toward us, I could see his ash-gray lab coat. It had designs and was rimmed in what looked like black silk. He walked gracefully in black metal-plated boots. His arms were crossed in front of his chest, with clenched fists—at least it looked like it. His face was expressionless. He had a thin mustache that was the same color as his lab coat, yet his hair and eyebrows were brownish gray. No family resemblance there.

Alexion's father stopped several feet away from us. He peered at us, wondering who we were, understandably. Maybe because I was with his son, a teenager holding a cello, a desperate AttackShift pilot who was holding a torch and a sword, a member of a completely different unnamed species, the Zerhali heir-not-to-be, and a Lyre who needed medical assistance. That's a lot to take in at one time.

But when the man finally spoke, it was in Russian. Alexion hesitantly went out from behind us. As he did, he turned and motioned for us—Augustine, Shyann, and I—to get down. Augustine obeyed, but I mouthed, *Why?*

"Just trust me," he said silently. "Get down."

So I did.

The three of us gently laid Ralloy down on the snow. He groaned softly. Masseran and Enstar backed up toward us and went on one knee beside us.

Alexion's father spoke in Russian and motioned in our general direction. Alexion turned back toward us and whispered, "My father wishes to have a translator, for he wants to speak in his own language yet wants you to hear clearly," he said with no expression. His face was ashen.

Augustine stood up. "I am capable of translating," he said, although he clearly wondered why he wanted this arrangement.

It looked like Alexion wanted to ask the same question himself, but he didn't. Alexion's father motioned for him to come, so the heir-not-to-be stood and waited for one of them to speak.

Alexion's father began. Augustine translated when he finished.

"So you escaped."

Alexion said nothing. He just looked down. Was he *more* than nervous? Did he feel shame? It was impossible for me to tell. But it was a dangerous time to ask.

Alexion's father continued. Translation: "After all that I tried, you still won't listen."

"The storm began," Alexion said quietly.

"But here you are. Right in front of me. In the company of Lindsair's family." Alexion's father kept pronouncing his Russian words as if he were from Earth's Far East region. "You have betrayed me more than twice. You have been a traitor every time you ever thought about them. Why do you come to me? Are you not ashamed to show for face before me?" He stepped forward and made Alexion step backward.

"The boy is in critical condition. He is in shock and has been for over an hour. He needs immediate help," the scientist pleaded.

His father stepped around him. "Did you believe that I would help a Lyre?" he asked.

"You are the closest available doctor! If he doesn't get treated soon, he will die!" Enstar shouted in response. Again, everyone was surprised by this, but Alexion's father gave a stern look.

"He is my enemy," Alexion's father replied in a thick Russian accent but in English.

"But doctors are supposed to help everyone, even their enemies!" Enstar pleaded. "I know! I'm a doctor too!"

This seemed to be going nowhere as Alexion's father gave a crooked grin. "Then I shall be the first to not," he said.

"But *please*, Father—"

"Do *not* call me Father." Alexion's father cut him off. Alexion shrank back. It was silent for a minute. Then he looked at us closely. "Who are you anyway? Why are you

134

here? Why did you come to me? Tell me, how do you know a Lyre, and why is he unconscious?" he asked suspiciously. Alexion moved aside, and his father stepped toward me. Why me in particular? I don't know.

Then he turned ninety degrees to the left when he was five feet away from Ralloy. "What if I …" he muttered. He stayed put, silent. Alexion just looked really nervous. His fretting over the storm seemed to be *nothing* compared to this. As least *then* he had an output. But now, anything he said could end off in a severe reprimand—or possibly worse. His father didn't give Alexion freedom of speech. Or any freedom at all.

Alexion suddenly began whispering in Russian again. He was almost silently speaking quickly at a pace his father likely couldn't follow. He was quivering. *He must know what his father is going to do.*

And then he didn't.

Alexion's father actually *didn't* actually *do* anything. He just turned and looked down at me. "I feel that you are afraid of me. Why would you want to give someone you obviously care about into the hands of a man you fear?" he asked me cryptically.

He has a point.

I don't know how to answer that.

Alexion's father took my silence as an answer. And maybe the fact that I was quivering, almost crying, cold, and indeed afraid of the doctor. He really had a point.

"As I thought. And not to add on the fact that if you are for the Liberators, I am your enemy, and you are mine," Alexion's father added on, certainly not improving the situation.

Is Alexion's father our last resort? Is he really *going to help us? He doesn't sound, look, or act like it. He seems to want to get as far away as possible from us or wants to do exactly what Zaphn was doing—or trying to do—with Shyann. Deprive us of hope.*

It sure was working. Enstar began crying again. Masseran dropped her cello and its bow. Augustine looked down with shaking shoulders. Alexion appeared to be crestfallen. Deprived of hope. Defeated. He whispered in Russian again, one sentence. I couldn't understand him, but I understood just the same.

We should not have come here.

It had not been long ago when we were in a similar circumstance. But this time, we were here willingly. This time, we were here on behalf of a life. Ralloy's life.

Chapter 22

Restoration

I LOOKED DOWN AT HIM. His eyes were closed now, but his chest still moved steadily. It was slower than normal. His chest wound hadn't grown, but it made him look worse. I felt his skin, but my fingers were numb. I couldn't tell how cold he was. But it was okay; what Ralloy needed to do was keep breathing. I hoped that he didn't receive lung damage from the heat stroke or his fall. Or from me—us—carrying him like that.

"I do not know in what condition Ralloy is in now, but I fear that he may be beyond human help at this point," Shyann said quietly. She was being honest, but it really didn't help.

"Then what was the point of all of this? Ralloy can't ..." I couldn't finish. If Alexion's father couldn't help, even if he would, then who?

It was too cold to cry. But I still felt like yelling at the sky like Enstar was. I had always been a silent mourner, but that didn't help. It really felt hopeless.

I felt a shift in the air. Shyann must be wing-signing, but as far as I was concerned, no one here understood them. Then she began whispering. "To whom will the victory go to?"

The same poem I had told Shyann before!

>"Light or darkness.
>The darkness forces;
>The light invites.
>It may appear at times that the dark is winning;
>That evil is stronger than good;
>But may I remind you, Ceriph,
>That it is the light that chases
>The shadows from all its corners?
>Yes, no matter how dark it may look
>The light will always be
>Victorious
>In the end."

My heart felt lighter as I took those words in. Yes, the light would win in the end.

"I understand how you are feeling, Ceriphina. I feel it too." Shyann sighed. "Defeat. But I would like to remind you that this isn't over yet. I can still detect a faint signal of energy from him—*life*. There is nothing that I can do, nor humans, to help. But he—all of us—still have even a microscopic amount of hope. No matter how tiny, hope is still present when He is present," she said softly.

That was comforting. Really.

I am sorry … Will you accept my apology … and … forgive me? He was suffering. Ralloy was so close to death that I couldn't hold his answer back.

"Ralloy ..." I began, trying to hold my tears back but failed. Tears of mine dropped slowly onto my dear friend's face. "I ... I ... You are ..." Why was this so hard to say?

"I hold nothing against you ... my friend. You are ... forgiven, Ralloy ..." I finally said. "Just stay alive ... Please ... Be okay ... healed ..."

Then I collapsed over him and wept.

I could hear the irregularity of Ralloy's heartbeat. His breaths were shallow. I lay there in full-fledged silence. No one spoke or moved. I heard Augustine softly break the silence by whispering in a different language, perhaps his native one. I guessed that the heir-not-to-be was praying. We really needed it right now. Alexion's father did not speak.

The silence returned for a second, then I heard more prayers being said. Augustine was continuing, and I heard everyone present except for a Russian accent. I knew Alexion's father was certainly *not* going to go with everyone's example, but I half expected Alexion himself to offer up a prayer even with his father near.

This continued for quite a while. A painfully long while. Eventually, the voices of my companions faded and stopped. Was it too late? I hadn't been paying attention to Ralloy's vital signs. I was trying to hear Alexion. Now I chose to look at them.

He was still alive. That's something worth celebrating by itself.

Ralloy *hadn't* gotten worse. He had actually *improved.* He felt warmer, not up to his normal of ninety-nine degrees but definitely not as cold as the surrounding snow. His heartbeat was stronger now, and his breaths were deeper and steadier.

I had a warm, stirring feeling inside and smiled. Happy tears flooded my closed eyes. Ralloy was healing, and God was doing it.

I felt a hand on the side of my head and upper ear rim. It was rather warm, and as I opened my eyes, I realized it was Ralloy's hand.

"Thanks," my friend whispered as if he was fragile.

"You are very, very welcome, Ralloy. Just … stay with us," I murmured back. "Please …"

Ralloy began stroking my hair. This was new from him, and I was perfectly fine with it. "Sure … I want to stay with you too … I'm supposed to protect you after all. I *want* to protect you," he replied softly. This was the first time Ralloy ever spoken to me this gently. Even as long as I had known him.

"Thanks." I said warmly. I rolled off Ralloy and onto the snow so he could breathe better. No less or more than I had completed a full rotation, though. The wind suddenly began strangely blowing the way we had come. The snow got a weird feeling too, as if it crystallized right below us. I instinctively rolled to get up on my feet.

"Stay down!" Alexion shouted and went down. His father seemed to have left. Everyone else dropped down as well. I laid on my back as a response, and immediately, a red object whirred dangerously above my face. It took me a second to figure out that it was a snowflake from the storm. But why was it red? Only the flakes closest to the energetic eye of the storm were red. Here, they were gray.

At least, they *were* gray. Not anymore, though. A look at the ground told me that the snow had changed colors too orangey-red. Scarlet.

What happened? How did the snowflakes change color? *Why* did they change color?

Enstar then raised Ralloy's sword to block a snowflake in Ralloy's direction. That either wasn't a good idea, or Enstar didn't have a very good grip, because the snowflake impacted the blade and sent it flying in Ralloy's direction. There has got to be a better move or a better outcome at this point, because Ralloy has risked his life enough times today.

We all watched the sword spin dangerously through the air toward my friend.

Chapter 23

Joy and Pain

RALLOY SAT UP AND GRABBED the sword in midair, seconds before it would have hit its mark.

Then he crouched and stayed low.

We all stared despite everything happening around us. How did he recover so fast?

Alexion visibly relaxed. Enstar just grinned happily. Masseran started up a quick cello solo that was pretty lively and joyful. Augustine was on his back and appeared grateful. We all might have been celebrating even more if we weren't in Setlia's most dangerous blizzard in history … by far.

I rolled onto my side, wanting to see Shyann. How did she show joy at this occasion?

I felt a tap on my back. I turned again and came face-to-face with Shyann. She was holding out the gentle torch in its baton state. She was trying to look glad, but she really couldn't hide the fact that she looked pained. As in hurt. She was also shedding strange transparent flakes. It wasn't taking anything off her, but it was strange. She was also trembling as if she was trying to survive an intense cold.

"What's wrong?" I asked instinctively. Before, only the appearance of Zaphn got her in a similar state, and *that* wasn't even *current*. And I was certain Zaphn wouldn't dare show *his* face here. It seems so dangerous he might not risk it. Ceiling is a whole other topic.

Shyann pushed the torch to me, so I put my hand on it. Then she looked at her chest. On her abdomen, there was a six-inch diagonal line. It wasn't bleeding, but the only thing that could have done that would be the … snowflakes. If that's true, then Shyann's armor *isn't* impenetrable … And the thing that can pierce her is bound to hurt painfully, *especially* because it's the snowflakes.

I grabbed hold of the gentle torch and looked at it. It wouldn't be a good idea to stand up and then turn it on.

So what if I turned it on and threw it in the air so it would possibly land on its point and avert the snowflakes, if that theory was still effective? If so, it might be narrower than before.

I turned and began army-crawling toward Ralloy. I thought I heard Shyann following, but I couldn't be sure. Once I reached him, I motioned for everyone else to huddle around. Half a minute passed as they gathered.

I went onto my back and began looking for a gap in the snowflakes. It wasn't hard to find as they were blowing right above us, and it was a very large gap, so I tossed the gentle torch up into it. It flew overhead and landed on its point. The torch then reverted to its torch state, standing on its end. The gentle flame blossomed and whipped around in the fierce wind, but it didn't blow out. The snowflakes dodged the torch, but the space was only large enough for three people side by side. The torch was five feet away from our entourage.

Then I heard someone sliding upon the snow. I turned my head to see who it was. My glance revealed that Shyann was moving toward the torch. The transparent scale-flakes were still peeling off, and she still looked freezing, but Shyann certainly was determined to at least reach the gentle torch. She was not letting her physical status bring her down or stop her.

Shyann was gaining ground as if she were a mountain climber, moving toward the torch as if she were ascending a cliff face. Her wings, which seemed so fragile now, were splayed, dragging in the snow beside her as she moved. Only three feet left until Shyann reached the gentle torch.

Two feet as my heart pumped faster and faster.

One foot as I began smiling.

And then …

Zero feet.

Shyann solidly grasped the gentle torch's base. She was silent for a second, then emitted what I guessed was a joyful shout. It was a little hard to tell, though.

I heard another shout of joy, this time obviously Enstar. I turned to see her, and she looked as excited as a little kid who got exactly what she wanted for Christmas. I honestly wouldn't have been surprised at this point if she jumped to her feet and started dancing suddenly if we weren't inside Setlia's most dangerous storm yet.

"Yes," I heard. I turned to Ralloy. His voice was stronger yet soft and gentle. He was certainly awake as he was on his stomach and watching avidly. And all that showed that he had recovered. Though it was the first time that he had ever spoken so gently, and I believed that it had more to do than lung weakness. Ralloy's experience definitely brought a major change—a good one.

I gave Ralloy a hug. He returned the embrace, and as he did, tears of joy ran down my cheeks. Ralloy was better again. Completely healed. Physically, emotionally, spiritually.

He slowly pulled his arm away and began army-crawling toward Shyann and the gentle torch. I followed, and the crunch of snow behind me told me that the others in our group were doing the same. Within thirty seconds, we all had gathered at the base of the torch, along with Shyann. Shyann let me hold the torch and moved to my left side, while Ralloy was on my right.

I fingered the base of the torch absentmindedly. Then I let go and went up on my knees hesitantly. The snowflakes were so close, too close.

After a minute though, I realized that they weren't coming any closer. The snowflakes, for whatever reason, couldn't come any closer to us or the gentle torch. The snowflakes could not touch me.

Realizing that gave me a surge of energy, and I stood boldly to my feet. The snowflakes seemed to shudder and move away when I did. I didn't question it. It only fueled my newfound determination. I gripped the gentle torch tightly.

As I looked behind and beside me, I saw that everyone else had done the same. Ralloy laid a hand on my shoulder, but it was Augustine who spoke to me.

"Onward, Ceriphina. Let us triumph over the storm!" he said. He was acting as if he had already won.

Definitely encouraging.

I lifted the torch from the ground easily.

Then I stepped forward, back into the depths and center of the storm of anger. I took one step after another …

Chapter 24

Triumph

I MARCHED CONFIDENTLY FORWARD. OUR path now strangely appeared to be narrowed to a certain path by a blue substance. Energy. A Pathway.

It only seemed like a matter of minutes, however, when the snowflakes grew larger and redder, like at the center of the storm. Only intensified.

After another minute, the tunnel energy vanished. I stopped and looked around. The snowflakes, if even possible, were moving faster and seemed to be dancing intricate patterns across the cloudy horizon. And our path.

But wait. There was a still snowflake, the one that all the others appeared to rotate around. The snowflake was a deep red, only the rim looking like actual ice. It was relatively small, compared to the rest of the snowflakes. It appeared to be a little imbalanced, for it hovered a few inches above ground, not quite parallel to the Setlian earth.

It must be the center of the storm of anger!

Augustine, Masseran, Enstar, and Alexion simultaneously grabbed the gentle torch and positioned their hands. Alexion suddenly let go and stared at his hands while stepping back. Masseran backed up, looked at me again, and turned to gaze intently to the left. Enstar moaned and put her hands on her forehead.

Shyann was over to the left, still shedding transparent flakes and struggling to carry someone I couldn't see.

The temperature rose as the torch jerked up, like someone had pushed or pulled it up.

We pushed down to keep it in place.

The torch stayed put, but it was trembling. It wasn't strong enough to withstand the pressure, but it somehow was holding it.

Stop resisting. I have a plan.

Then little indigo blips appeared out of nowhere around our feet and zoomed straight toward Shyann.

No, not Shyann—the other invisible person Shyann was carrying!

I watched helplessly. What else could I do? What *are* they in the first place? Are they attacks or something else?

The blips inevitably hit the form who lost her cloak of invisibility when they hit.

The form looked exactly like a Barshal that was on fire!

Whatever the blips were, the Barshal was visibly shocked. The hesitation gave Shyann the opportunity to get a good grip and soar straight to the torch's flame.

Time seemed to slow down in that moment. The temperature soared to its peak.

I caught a glimpse of the Barshal's piercing gaze.

The Barshal was Moraiha!

My jaw dropped open. Why were Shyann and Moraiha … ? Did they know each other?

The torch was moved even further up. We all resisted and pushed down. It felt like we were getting nowhere. Shyann was coming closer, and the gentle torch must be buckling.

If the torch didn't move fast enough, Shyann was so focused so that she couldn't turn away from the direction she was flying in. She would hit the flame, and I don't know what would happen then.

What if it actually helped Shyann? Then right before Shyann and Moraiha hit the flame, the opposition was suddenly gone. The torch now was going down. It made a clean hole through the snowflake. Right when Shyann passed through the gentle flame.

Chapter 25

Symbolic Aftermath

EVERYTHING WENT WHITE AS SHYANN did and stayed white. I felt like I was floating, and when I looked down, it proved to be true. Just like in my dream last night.

So I looked to the left, and the statue from my dream was there. The javelin-arrow was there, still embedded in its chest. But the red lines I clearly remembered were gone. They simply weren't there anymore.

Was my dream … real? This clearly wasn't Setlia. I feel like it *transcends* science. This is beyond explanation.

Then I saw Ralloy. He wore the same uniform as the statue, only with the tears and wounds on him. He moved closer to the statue, closer until he reached it. He placed his hand on the javelin-arrow, tightly.

Then in one fluid motion, the young warrior pulled the javelin-arrow out of the statue's chest.

I slowly went over to him. It was all clear to me now. The statue was supposed to represent Ralloy. The three arrows were representing the three things that were taken from him during the Terrible Raid—the EIC, Oeilla, and his older sister Marsara. The taking of the EIC was the quill-arrow, the taking of Oeilla was the second arrow, and the taking of Marsara was the third arrow. The javelin-arrow. The wound that hurt the most and festered the most, giving way to anger and bitterness. Ralloy had harbored the pain from the loss of his sister all these years but never let it out. He kept it hidden under an all-too-transparent mask. The storm of anger was his incredibly dangerous way of releasing it.

And this was Ralloy's way of saying, "I'm sorry. I was wrong to do this. For making everyone suffer. I am so very sorry."

Ralloy never said a word. He took a deep breath. Several of them. The javelin-arrow in his grasp disintegrated.

Then he drew his blade, free of orange arcs. There was no intense heat emanating from him. The young warrior fingered the hilt, looking at it as if it was his first time seeing it. Maybe he was seeing the weapon in a new set of eyes. Like everything else Ralloy knew. He would have a different outlook.

How I knew this is because I knew that this time Ralloy was giving a promise.

And this promise was genuine.

Ralloy raised the sword in the air above his head. "Let's win this battle," he whispered.

It looked like the sky flickered, and then we were suddenly surrounded by Alexion, Augustine, Enstar, Masseran, and Shyann. Shyann was the only one who appeared to know what happened to some degree. Everyone else looked at us like, *What just happened?*

Suddenly, a squad of helicopters—from the Alsekan side, it looked—flew overhead. They were returning to Alseka. One of them appeared damaged and wobbled in flight as smoke and sparks poured out of the side of it.

"I think that it would be best if we go back to Varnillon before one of those helicopters detect us," Shyann suggested.

Ralloy turned around and began climbing to the summit without a word. After a moment, Alexion followed him. Then went everyone else, but Augustine stayed with me.

The heir-not-to-be looked out to the right of the near peak of Mount Thias. North, where his homeland of Zerhal lay. Was he thinking about Zinnune?

"Why would you want to be with someone that was avoiding you? You have risked much for Ralloy ... much more than was asked of you. More than I expected. You did something today that I haven't been able to do. Move. I couldn't react with my brother, but you risked everything for the life of your ... friend. I know that you wouldn't have done any of this if all you wanted was a conversation with Ralloy. I think I know why ... but I want you to tell me, Ceriphina. What was your motivation?" Augustine asked, turning back to face me. He placed his hand on my shoulder. "Why did you risk your very life for someone who didn't want anything to do with you before?" The heir-not-to-be looked at me genuinely. He really wanted to know.

"Why, Ceriphina?" Augustine asked a third time. His hand dropped from my shoulder to my hand. "Why."

My answer was simple. "Because I care for Ralloy. And I love him like a brother," I answered just as genuinely as Augustine's question.

Augustine smiled. "Ruofen was right about you, Ceriphina. I have seen few young women with a heart so bold," he said to me.

I smiled as well. "Thank you, Augustine. Thank you for everything."

"Thank you, Ceriphina. I just want you to know that I am very grateful for you." Augustine shed a few tears. He wiped them away. These were not tears of sorrow. They were tears of joy. Of gratitude.

I felt my eyes water too.

After a minute, Augustine let go of my hand. "Let's go back now."

He led me carefully to the top of the mountain. Shyann was waiting for us there. The others must have went back to Varnillon. There weren't any more helicopters in the air. Funny. The city was partially destroyed as I looked over it. There were both crashed AttackShift aircraft and enemy helicopters on the ground.

But no more helicopters came. No Exposial dragons were to be seen, and no sign of enemy conquest. Varnillon's flag was raised high in the center of the city, tattered, torn, and dirty, but still in the air, visible for all in the city to see.

"The battle has ended. Varnillon is victorious, and Alseka, with the Oppression, have failed to conquer. It will be some time before they decide to attack. The battle is won, though," Shyann stated.

The last words of the poem came back to me. "Yes, no matter how dark it may look, the light will always be victorious in the end."

I felt relieved. For the time being, we were safe. Even on the Border Mount. The Lord Almighty will surely protect us.

We descended to Varnillon slowly and thoughtfully. We reached the city in fifteen minutes. Augustine and Shyann went over to Ruofen's tent on the other side of the city via a Pathway. I walked down the charred road by myself. After a few turns in the road, I saw Ralloy looking at the remains of a burnt house. I glanced around the street, realizing that this was our neighborhood. My house was in the same condition as Ralloy's—destroyed.

I looked at Ralloy again. He looked at the rubble that was his home. The young warrior was noticeably not angry. No yelling. No "Why did this have to happen?" at the sky. No see-through facade. No nothing. He was just standing there.

I slowly approached him. I didn't know how he would react, but he just nodded once when I neared. Then Ralloy turned to face me.

Silently, he looked at the ground for a moment. I waited for him to speak.

"Ceriphina … it would be an honor to call you my friend once more." Ralloy looked up at me. He didn't say anything else. He didn't need to.

I walked over to him, and I threw my arms around Ralloy and embraced him. Ralloy was visibly surprised by this, but I meant it. I really did love him like a brother. And I had missed him. That was why I kept going back, trying to be with him.

And then Ralloy returned the embrace. He wrapped his arms lightly around me. Finally, peace between us. Reconciliation.

"Thank you, Ceriph," Ralloy responded. No more was said. Nothing needed to be. All could be felt in that moment.

Finally, Ralloy released me, and I did the same. Ralloy smiled, a true, honest smile. I returned it.

"It looks like we might have to go back to the border camp," he said. Ralloy started down the burned street. I followed him. Happily.

"Ceriphina?" I suddenly heard from behind. I turned around and saw it was Ruofen. How did he get here?

"Well done, Ceriph," Ralloy's father said. "Well done."

Epilogue

Lindsair

November 30
1:30 PM

THE OPPRESSION HAVEN'T ATTACKED VARNILLON again, although other cities close to the border have been assaulted. I moved in with Ralloy in the general's tent since I don't have a place to go. Emayne was at the camp during the battle, and wasn't physically hurt by her home burning down. The tent is crowded as Enstar and Masseran with her cello were staying with us. We are living in multiple tents because of space.

Augustine had decided to go back to Zerhal, back to his home, a few days after the battle. The lockdown would likely be lifted for the day he returns. He gave me his frequency to call and message him for when he got to the real Norheil castress. We've been doing it often, me using one of the guest computers Ruofen had. He has more than I expected.

Alexion decided to go with the heir-not-to-be, which wasn't all too surprising. He never said it, but I'm certain that Alexion wants to put as much ground and ocean between him and his father as possible.

And Shyann mysteriously disappeared a week ago. I didn't think she left on her own accord. It was impossible to tell where she was now even with Varnillon's best energy radars. Shyann had gone missing, like Sane, without a trace. Only this time, there was no complicated computer program that held a barely interoperable clue where she was.

I haven't seen Moraiha ever since the storm.

Now I was on the border of the Varnillon border camp, watching the ragged path up the Border Mount. Nobody really used it, but I had the feeling that I should expect someone. Not sure who, but Ralloy's sitting with me too. He's been quiet lately, so we just sit together when he wants to. It's still awkward to talk about things, mostly because I may not be the best conversation starter when it comes to small talk, but at least we were together.

I checked the low-range energy radar in my hand. It had a twelve-foot radius, and now I saw something. It was a signal similar to Ralloy's, seven feet away, but Ruofen and Enstar were inside the camp. I heard that the main radars at the city hall had picked up a Lyre signal like this one a couple days ago, but it was too fast, and no one could investigate it.

I looked up, and there was a man climbing the rarely used path. He did have the red hair that everyone in the Lyre family had, and he was dressed for the Arctic. He was wearing an extra layer and heavy-duty boots. A scabbard was at his side, as well as what looked like a baton.

I don't think he's Enstar's dad, because he would be flying a helicopter, not walking. He would also have given us a message saying he was coming.

As the man neared, I heard two pairs of footsteps from behind me. I turned and saw that it was Ruofen and Enstar.

Ruofen looked surprised, and it looked like it was because of the visitor.

The man waved his hand hesitantly at Ruofen. The general looked stunned for a second, then rushed carefully down the outcrop I was sitting on, then down the path the man was on. Ralloy stood and followed his father, and Enstar did the same. I carefully lowered myself from the outcrop and walked over to the gathering of Lyres.

Ruofen was hugging the man, who looked like he wasn't quite prepared for it. The man was smaller than Ruofen, not having the same muscular frame that the general had. Ralloy and Enstar were observing. The man had longer hair than Ruofen's.

When Ruofen let go of the man, the man began to speak. "I wasn't expecting this, Ruofen," he said, bewildered.

"What were you expecting? That I would turn you away?" Ruofen replied, smiling.

"No. I don't really know what I was expecting. Just not this." The man smiled back.

"Well, come on in! The city was half destroyed in the battle, so we all have been camping out in tents," Ruofen said.

"Okay. Yours is green, right?" the visitor guessed. Ruofen laughed, then began walking to his tent. We all followed, and I was wondering who the man was.

Emayne and Masseran were surprised when we returned with a guest. Especially Emayne. She seemed a little nervous about him. The man noticed. So did Ruofen.

The man unfastened his belt and laid it on the ground. Emayne relaxed a little. Masseran looked like she was wondering why the man did that.

"I see a couple of faces I don't recognize here. May I introduce myself?" the man asked. Ruofen nodded.

"All right. For the two young ladies here … I am Lindsair."

And that explained Ruofen's reaction. And why he took his belt off.

I realized that Lindsair had the same attitude as Augustine—repentant. But what Lindsair did, he did years ago. Ruofen had been worried about his brother ever since he left the Oppression. And now he's here, and Ruofen was happy.

"Why did you decide to come, Lindsair?" Ruofen asked his brother.

"For one thing, I wanted to see you and your family. But I'm following Listen," Lindsair said.

"And you think he went through here?"

"Yes. He was on a magnetic transport module that had its trajectory go through here to Zerhal," Lindsair told us. Magnetic transport modules only go in one direction, and if it was going to Zerhal …

"Listen was in Alseka," Ruofen concluded. "But why? He has no reason to be there."

"Listen misunderstood the meaning of 'traitor twice,'" Lindsair explained. "I think he thought that he had to go back. He's impulsive, but I'm certain that he wants to come home now."

"Where is your home?" Ruofen asked. "And why did the Oppression send him to Zerhal, since he's your son?"

"Technology and leadership aren't his strong points. So he could be on prison duty, but in the Arctic? It still confuses me," Lindsair admitted.

I'll ask Augustine about that later.

"So that's why I'm here. Can you explain why half of Varnillon is living in tents? You said there was a battle," Lindsair prompted.

"Oh, there was a battle, all right. Let's all tell the story together, okay?" Ruofen gathered everyone, and Emayne left to another tent. "It began on the first of this November ..."

Lindsair gave Ruofen a frequency to contact him if necessary. This is what it was:

OPL
KZX_AL-1.03
FREC.
Ceriphina
Sent to Augustine, Freq. 72.8 FAR_N 4:43 PM,
Nov. 30

Hidden Chapter

1

Shyann
November 22
3:18 AM

THE NIGHT WAS STILL. NOT even a breeze tinged the dark sky. Instinctively, I was reminded of the calm before the storm and how well that was utilized earlier in November. But Zaphn was far from Varnillon, though I felt a presence that lingered lowly. I kept my watch steady anyway, as it felt too calm tonight to relax. I had woken up a while ago, restless, so I had decided to do a night watch to make sure everyone was all right.

It was also rather warm for November on a mountain. Snow had fallen the day before, so it should have been around twenty to forty degrees. But it felt like sixty degrees. Why was that? Another impossible storm, as Ceriphina calls it? Or did the storm of anger put the weather off kilter?

Or could it be an energetic threat? It was likely, with Ceriphina's energy trace. But of course, I was more of a threat to the Oppression than Ceriphina, but her connections to the Lyre family may prove her to be quite ... strong. In multiple ways.

I heard snow shift behind me, and I whirled around silently. I saw nothing. It could have been melting due to the heat, but I felt that something—no, someone—was here. With not necessarily good intentions. I kept my observance.

No more snow moved. I concentrated on the spot, slowly stepping closer. I still saw nothing.

Then I felt something suddenly zero in on me—not Ceriphina—from behind. I spun around quickly to face ... Nothing? I now *felt* surrounded but still could see no one. Was there someone who was messing with my energetic perceptions? I slowly and frantically turned around. Still nothing.

This makes no sense. No sense at all.

Suddenly, I felt no threat. There appeared to be no one energetically close by.

What? No threat moves that fast. So my perceptions *are* being played with ... But who would do that? Zaphn. It was possible. But to attempt to trick me into thinking I was surrounded? That seems to be too much at this point, as I had actually gotten as close as one can get to beating him in energetic combat. It seemed unlikely he would try to even get close.

So this must be a new opponent. But who?

I readied myself for an attack. I unfurled my wings for aerial combat, and my fists were prepared to unleash a very powerful attack. Or perhaps a Shield. Yet I held back, waiting for the enemy to show itself.

Then I felt a hand on my shoulder. My tension went higher, for the hand really felt like metal and at the same time like a dragon's. But under those, I felt a very powerful stirring, but not a helpful one. I had only heard of it, but at this stage, I should have expected it. But I was frightened all the same.

The hand held DragonWave, an immense energy force; it was the core of the Oppression. And the Oppression wanted me badly.

I stiffly turned around to face the holder, but my confidence was gone. It zoomed to the negatives when I realized it was made of Condensed Shadow, which I had never fought against. From what I had heard (which was very little), Condensed Shadow was immune to most energetic attacks. And all physical attacks. I glanced around, and it didn't help much, as I saw now I actually was surrounded by more figures of Condensed Shadow. I dropped my stance, lowered my wings, and raised my internal guard.

My heart dropped as I noticed that the figures were conversing. My body wanted to faint and be over with it, but my mind and heart argued that that would be exactly what the enemy wanted. I had to stay awake, even if I was warring against myself.

The DragonWave was coming in the energetic play now, like the ocean at high tide, except faster. I didn't show any external fear, but my vision was beginning to whiten. I tried to force myself to at least take one step forward. Little determination didn't help as the Condensed Shadow had an ironic grip like iron."

The figures seemed to be done talking in their language that I didn't understand.

Then they spoke in standard English.

And I understood perfectly.

"SHALL WE BEGIN?"
"YES, LET US UNLEASH THE TSUNAMI!"

I almost did faint. I barely remembered what happened next. But I clearly know the result.

Hidden Chapter

2

UNEXPLORED TERRITORY, FAR FAR NORTH,

---. --

--:-- --

Arocia

THE COLD ARCTIC HEADWIND BLEW my mane away as I sat, watching the south. I had felt something was coming for a while, but I wasn't sure who or what it was. Something dangerous, I knew, but somehow different than the civil war we had fled. Something more potent, maybe. But it was unfamiliar, and it was certainly the enemy. Just not one we had seen before.

But why would they attack us when we were this far north? There were better opportunities when we were still among the chaos of the war. It didn't quite line up...

But we were isolated now. Just me, Alphastar, Omegablast, Acolbei, who was Alphastar's mate, Berquius,

Cassiiron, Alabaster, and Alphastar's two-year-old daughter Maifore were hiding out in the bitter reaches of the Far Far North. Easier to target, but where else were we supposed to go? Home was no longer home, and Berquius' family was the farthest from the war we could go. And as far as I knew, the rest of the world was caught up in their own war, so how could it safer? We were away from warring civilizations, Alphastar said. War destroyed civilizations, and we had fled, so we would not be destroyed.

But Alphastar had been hurt by the war. The people had rebelled under him, and there was now an underlying bitterness about him. What did it matter, if we were the last of our kind? That was how he felt, even if he never said it.

Something stirred, a long way south. I stiffened and stood to my full height, a little over eleven feet. I peered south, trying to see the enemy from this far. They were out of sight, but I felt that they weren't the "enemies" we were used to. Were they maybe from the other war that the rest of Setlia was in? Maybe. And I didn't recognize the energy that was approaching.

I was there for a while, trying to figure this out. Finally, I could see something on the horizon. Was it a cloud? It was a dark... mist, it seemed like. As it speeded closer, I saw fighter jets I recognized from the south. None of my kind used jets at all, so the threat was definitely from the world's war.

I turned around. "Alphastar! There's definitely something coming from the south!" I shouted to an obscured mountain cave entrance. "And it's from the other war!"

Alphastar and Omegablast ducked out of the cave, the entrance being a little too small for them. "Do you know what they have?" Alphastar asked me.

"Jets and a weird mist. They're too far off for me to tell if they have anything else." I told him.

"At least we don't have to be careful, then." Cassiiron poked his head out of the cave.

"You know what he meant." Alabaster squeezed through and gave his brother a look. "We have to be careful not to get killed, Cassiiron."

Alphastar went rigid for a second at killed. Then he relaxed and set his eyes on the horizon. Acolbei had stayed inside with little Maifore, but Berquius joined us. We were ready.

But I had a little feeling that we weren't.

The jets began firing as they neared us. We Shielded, and sprang into flight. We quickly caught up to the jets, but there were only three of them. That struck me as odd. Was there some more in the mist? Or something else?

Alphastar formed his sword and cleaved the nose off one of the jets. Cassiiron did the same, but stuck his sword into the plane as if to prove that he was stronger. Pure Cassiiron. I lunged at the remaining jet and grabbed its wing. As it wobbled, I slowly crushed its metal wing. I then tossed it aside, looking to the mist that had traveled slower than the jets. Too easy.

Omegablast had been behind us, and as I looked at him, I saw that he had a grim look on his face. There was clearly something up, and Omegablast saw it.

Cassiiron, not so much. "Did you see that?" he said, apparently thrilled for some reason. Both Alabaster and Alphastar gave him an annoyed look.

"I see that mist, though. Know what it is?" Alabaster retorted.

"Why do you think I know?"

"I don't."

Both brothers sighed. This was common for them.

"Look!" Omegablast pointed suddenly. We did, and the mist had stopped advancing. Now, we could see Exposial dragons coming out of it. One in particular was in front of them all, with quite a mark on his left cheek. That one roared, and the Exposials behind him zoomed towards us.

I Shielded, and a few of them just bumped into me. Alphastar took several down, and Cassiiron followed his example. Everyone else tried, but there were so many of them. And the one that had roared went straight for me.

I rammed my Shield into him as he flew towards me. The Exposial dragon pushed against it, but my strength matched his. So we were there for a minute, until another Exposial slammed into me and pulled me to the ground. He detached himself from me before I hit, but I couldn't regain my balance. The leader Exposial landed in front of me, and offered a strange sort of smile. Not a nice one.

"Ahh, so we meet at last, Aiethawn." he said.

"Who are you, and why are you here? Don't you have your own war?" I questioned, clenching my fists.

"I am Zaphn." the Exposial said. "And I am under orders."

Then he lunged at me. I sidestepped, noticing that Omegablast was also on the ground, surrounded. Five more Exposial dragons landed around me, and I reinforced my Shield. The Exposials outnumbered us. They outnumbered me. No wonder we weren't ready.

The Exposial leader Zaphn lunged at me again. I backed into another, who grabbed my wings, keeping me grounded. I struggled, kicking at the Exposial's shins. My wings were twisted as a result, arching my back in pain. I refused to groan. "What do you want?" I asked Zaphn.

His eyes narrowed. "It is of no concern to you, Aiethawn." he growled.

"I concur, if you came all the way up here. It is my concern." I returned.

Zaphn gave a quiet roar, then placed his head close to mine. So close, I could see the damage to the scales on his left cheek. "Just be quiet." he whispered harshly to me. Then he grabbed my arms and pulled me close to him. This motion hurt my shoulders badly, and neither dragon let go. Still, I didn't cry out, although I was about to. Zaphn squeezed my forearms tightly.

Suddenly, I felt a strange and draining energy emanate from Zaphn's claws. I tried to pull away again, but the Exposial with a grip on my wings twisted even more. I finally cried out, for it was too much to hold in at this point. Zaphn tightened his grip, and I saw a light purple glow from the point of contact. I tried to fight it still, but now it was arcing, entering the cracks in between my scales. My breathing grew more labored as the same weakening force entered me though my wings. What... is it? I was wondering as the Exposials released me.

"It has been done." I heard Zaphn whisper. I struggled to stand upright as the dragons left me. The weakening force had spread fast, and the world was slightly off-kilter. Before I fell to the ground, I released the loudest roar I could. It wasn't that strong, but it was something.

Then the world went dark.

I awoke to a long roar. I slowly sat up, and the world came back into focus. Alabaster was there, and he helped me to my feet. I could see Berquius and Cassiiron struggle to stand, too. The Exposials were gone.

Alphastar roared again. I turned to see him, and his strands of fire erupted from his short red mane. They blazed fiercely, telling us that Alphastar was angry. I looked around, unsure of why the Aiethawn was so upset.

As Alphastar unleashed a third roar, I suddenly realized that Omegablast was gone. Taken away by the Exposial dragons that had come this far north. Omegablast wasn't here anymore.

And Alphastar was unapproachable.

Glossary

Age of Conquest. The ten-year period of time before the Liberators' War, when the Oppressor was rising to power.

Alexion. Russian scientist who was forced to design the storm of anger.

Alexiov. Alexion's birth name.

Alseka. The mega-nation, the center of Setlia's development. Also heavily guarded in case of a less-than-likely rebellion.

AttackShift aircraft. A manned aircraft meant for battle. They have parts that are only connected to the craft by controlled magnetism, and the pilot can command the aircraft to shift the magnets to attack another aircraft, hence the name.

Augustine. Skilled warrior and son to the king of Zerhal who expected to be the heir.

Barnillon. Organization that conducted the Terrible Raid.

Barshal. A Setlanic species that migrated to Setlia. There is only one known at the time.

Bengial. The ruler of Caredest who is indecisive in whether he is king (monarchy) or president (democracy). The governor decided on monarchy for him since he has been in office for several years with no election.

Caredest. The relatively small northern nation that shares southwest a border with Alseka, the Oppressor's stronghold. Considered one of Alseka's greatest threats.

castress. A cross between a castle and a fortress. They can rise in a day since they are usually made with cybersteel.

Ceriph. Ceriphina's nickname used by those close to her.

Ceriphina. Ralloy's across-the-street neighbor who attempts to make things right with Ralloy.

Condensed Shadow. Beings that the Oppressor uses when he wants someone in particular, entirely.

cybersteel. Computer-controlled steel used mostly as a building material.

DragonWave. A controlling energy that the Oppression uses when there is a warrior they want on their side.

energy. The power generated by the energetic field that is generated by Setlia, by theory. Energy is used as a tool, but in more cases than not, as a weapon.

energy trace. A term with two meanings. The first is an energetic beacon signaling the presence of the person it is placed on. The term can also be interchangeable with energy signal.

Emayne Lyre. Ruofen's wife and family doctor.

Enstar Lyre. Excellent AttackShift pilot and swordmaiden and Ralloy's cousin.

Exposial. A type of dragon with the ability to Probe but can only do so if the target is willing or unconscious. Often the target is not willing, because the Exposials are forceful and are powerful in energetic and physical combat.

Gate. A Pathway to another dimension.

Ilde. The military and political capital of Alseka.

Liberators. The resistance to the Oppression, who lost their own war.

Liberators' War. A war that began 311 years ago that defined the lines of the Oppression and the Liberators. The war has continued to wage, until the 300-year mark, when the

THE STORM OF ANGER

Oppression executed the final move of the war, conquering the vast majority of Setlia and finally defeating the Liberators, as it looked at the time. Caredest and Zerhal remain the two nations that are still under their own leadership.

Lindsair Lyre. Ruofen's younger brother who doesn't visit but has a valid reason.

Listen Lyre. Lindsair's adult son who didn't inherit his father's skill with computers and technology.

Masseran. Sixteen-year-old mathematical genius who was coerced into doing the mathematics of the storm of anger by the Barnillon.

Moraiha. A female Barshal.

Norheil castress. The fortress-palace of the Zerhali king. Built of stone.

Oeilla. Zynkosiac who was ill and dear to Ralloy. She was taken during the Terrible Raid, and Ralloy has been angry ever since.

Oppression. The Oppressor's army that won the Liberators' War.

Oppressor. The man who leads the Oppression against the Liberators and rules Alseka with an iron fist.

Pathway. A way of quick transport through space and matter that can only be accessed by energy. It is similar to a portal but is more complex in navigating factors. Pathways are temporary shortened energy tunnels that can only be used in the same dimension.

Probe. The Exposial dragons' specialized way of retrieving information from others. The Exposial mentally Probes the mind of the holder of information and obtains it with the established temporary mental connection.

Ralloy Lyre. Fourteen-year-old warrior who was the victim of the Terrible Raid.

Razorwood grove. The small space in between Varnillon and the slope of Mount Thias. It is covered in bramble-like trees, thus the name.

Rei. Augustine's younger sister who disappeared a few years ago.

Ruofen Lyre. Ralloy's father and the general of Caredest's military.

Sane. Ceriphina's adopted older brother. He went missing five weeks ago on November 1.

Sanova. Augustine's older sister who disappeared a few years ago.

Setlan. A neighboring planet farther from the sun than Setlia. A recent event caused all on the planet to be destroyed, but the event and what caused it remain unknown.

Setlia. The planet in war.

Shyann. The only known person of Species X.

telasclisior. The feeling someone with a placed energy trace on them in place of sight.

Varnillon. The small city built close to the summit of the Border Mount, Mount Thias, on the Caredest side of the border.

Zerhal. A small nation nestled safely in the Arctic Protection Zone. Targeted as one of Alseka's greatest threats due to its Liberator alliance.

Zinnune. The heir to the throne of Zerhal and Augustine's younger brother.

Zynkosiacs. A species that has lived in harmony with the residents of Mount Thias. They fly most of the time, often in small groups, but when the Border Mount is under attack, they assist and group up altogether and help neutralize the enemy.

How a Seventh Grader Wrote a Full-Fledged Book

THIS SERIES STARTED OFF A little complicated. It sort of started with my graphic novel in fourth grade. The setting was various islands. The island background came in again in my first book attempt, *The Setlian Dragon Masters*. Now in the Liberators' War II series, I am still using Setlia.

I began writing The Royal Dragon Chronicles (predecessor to Liberators War II) in the summer before sixth grade, actually *before* I got the idea for *The Storm of Anger*. Ironic, isn't it? So it was going well (relatively) until the next summer. I never finished the original manuscript for the first book, *Alpheus*, or *Alpheus Greets Bravery*. Same story in either case. The first book in Liberators' War II branches off the idea.

Anyway, back to the reason I decided to write this section in the first place. How I was able to do this as a seventh grader. I started over the summer of transitioning schools on my family computer. I got up to about halfway on chapter 2. I took it to Grandma's house a few times. It was slow-going.

So over the summer, I got a phone. I'm not a heavy phone user. What I used most on my phone was Google Docs to present to you the prequel to Liberators' War II and *Against the Deceiver*. What you are reading right now, I typed on my phone.

So of course, it continued into school. I worked on it after school and during breaks, not during passing periods. I worked on it at any time I could. It was pretty interesting. So thus, it progressed into this book or novel or whatever you want to call it. Whatever it's called. I'm settling with novel.

Now, the end. Since part of the book was on the computer (Word) and most on my phone (Google Docs) on two accounts, my dad and I decided to transfer the majority of the story and the other needed parts on Google Docs to the beginning of the story from Word. So I could only edit the whole thing on the computer. That wasn't working well. So we transferred everything to Google Docs on one account. Again.

Then I pretty much rewrote almost the whole thing mostly on the computer since I was having difficulty on my phone.

I also drew the pictures by hand.

About the Author

REBECCA JIRU IS A TWELVE-YEAR-OLD seventh grader who resides in Santa Clarita, California. At third grade, becoming an author at age twelve was the last thing she wanted. Rebecca strongly disliked writing and even abbreviated her sentences. Do not do that ever. The principal will talk to you and your parents. She was placed into the Creative Writing Contest and surprisingly won third place of the third-grade participants. Two years later, Rebecca tried again, actually trying to win because she enjoyed writing and was actually writing a real book (this is not the original book from then; this is an advancement of it) that differed from her graphic novel in fourth grade. She won second place, but never finished the book. The next year, in sixth grade, she tried again, both in book and contest. She entered the contest under awkward circumstances, and this was the year that she won it. The book attempt went well, but Rebecca paused it in exchange for *The Storm of Anger*. This is the first time she has ever finished a novel, and the paused book, with many improvements, will be the first installment in the Liberators' War II series. The book is titled *War for Alphastar.*

Rebecca has two parakeets named Awana and Timothy. Her younger brother also has two parakeets named Markus and Noel.

Also, I would like to thank Mrs. Tredick, Mrs. Hubbard and Mrs. Pithey for their encouragement.

CPSIA information can be obtained
at www.ICGtesting.com
Printed in the USA
FSHW02n1034010518
47652FS